A COWBOY

FOR

CHRISTMAS

Susan Fisher-Davis

A Callahan Novella

Erotic Romance

A Cowboy for Christmas
Copyright © 2016 Susan Fisher-Davis
First Print book Publication: February 2019
ISBN: 978-1797047911
Cover design by Untold Romance and Fantasy Covers
All cover art copyright © 2016 by Susan Fisher-Davis

PUBLISHER:
Blue Whiskey Publishing

Acknowledgements

To Toby Schuler, Dedee Hayes, and Kelli McCleeary for being the best beta readers out there.

To all of you reading this book.

Thank you for your support. I appreciate it more than you know.

Prologue

Reid Callahan stared at the casket and still found it hard to believe that his best friend was inside it. Pain ripped through his heart at the thought of losing Zeke. They'd grown up together and had become the best bull riders on the circuit, both winning buckles and taking first place from each other. A small, sad smile lifted his lips as he remembered how they'd competed against each other, but always supporting one another. They were happy for each other's success. For years, they rode the circuit together...until Zeke met Lucy and fell in love. Hard.

Reid lifted his gaze to see Lucy standing on the other side of the casket, tears streaming down her cheeks. She raised her eyes to his and all he saw there was pure hatred. She blamed him for this and he knew she'd never forgive him. He just wanted Zeke to go one more time and look where that had gotten him. His best friend was dead now and Lucy hated him for it.

He shifted his eyes away from her. It hurt too much to look at her. She was a stunning woman with long, dark brown hair and beautiful light blue eyes. She had a pert nose that sat over the most sensual pair of lips he'd ever seen. He'd fallen in love with her the day Zeke introduced him to her soon after they started dating. Reid blew out a breath and watched it form into a puff of cold air. Rain beat down on his Stetson and poured off the brim to land on his boots. The rain seemed perfect for the day, and the way he was feeling.

When the service was over, Reid couldn't get his feet to move to walk away. Damn it. This should never have happened. Zeke was too good. Reid closed his eyes as the image replayed in his head yet again.

Zeke had given him the thumbs up as he straddled the bull, ready to ride. He'd drawn Firecracker...the meanest bull on the circuit. No cowboy had ever ridden him the full eight seconds but if anyone could, it was Zeke. Reid had watched as Zeke lowered himself onto the bull's back, gave the nod, and then the chute door opened. Firecracker shot out into the open immediately bucking and roaring, trying his best to dislodge the rider from his back. The bull rocked him first to the left and then back to the right. The clock was nearly at *six seconds*. Reid was positive Zeke was going to do it...until Firecracker jumped high, and kicked out. Zeke flew off hitting the sawdust-covered ground. The crowd groaned along with Reid. He stood on the rails and yelled for Zeke to run. Zeke got to his feet to run, but Firecracker was on him with his head down aiming for him.

Zeke ran toward the rails but Firecracker caught him, and tossed him with his horns. Zeke hit the ground again, but got to his feet as quickly as he could. The rodeo clowns had done their best to distract the bull, but he was having none of it. He was only interested in getting to the rider who'd had the balls to get on his back. He caught Zeke right before he reached the rails.

Reid put his hand out to his friend. He saw the pure terror on Zeke's face as he reached his hand out to Reid, but Firecracker rammed him into the fence. Reid remembered the loud groan that emerged from his friend as he fell to the ground. Trapped with nowhere to go, Firecracker gored Zeke tossing him over his head.

Everything seemed to happen in slow motion to Reid as he jumped the rail to get to his friend. At that moment, he hadn't given a shit about the bull or the danger. He needed to get to Zeke. Firecracker stood over Zeke as if he'd just won a trophy. He looked up as Reid ran toward him and back to Zeke, and then stomped on his chest with a hoofed foot. The rodeo clowns had finally gotten Firecracker away from him as Reid reached Zeke. He lifted his friend's limp body and ran to the fence. The rodeo doctor had him lay Zeke on a stretcher, which someone quickly rolled to an ambulance in the back of the arena. Reid had stayed beside the stretcher holding Zeke's hand.

Reid had climbed into the ambulance just as Lucy arrived. He helped her inside and they rode to the hospital together. Zeke was alive, but barely. Reid and Lucy both had tears rolling down their faces, neither wanting to believe any of this was actually happening.

Thirty minutes later, Zeke was gone. Reid had stood stoically beside Lucy as the doctor told them there was nothing he could do to save him. There had been internal bleeding that they couldn't stop. Lucy nearly fell to her knees but Reid caught her, and held her while she sobbed. After a few minutes, she gazed up at him with tears glistening on her long lashes. Her face went from sorrow to hatred in seconds. She pushed away from him.

"Don't touch me. This is your fault, Reid Callahan. You're the one who will have to live with this. You killed your best friend, and my husband. I hope you rot in hell," she'd told him, and then walked back to the room where Zeke lay on a gurney.

Reid had felt sucker punched. She blamed him, hated him, and swore she'd never forgive him. Thing was, she was probably right. He never should have talked Zeke into one more ride. *Fuck!*

He shook the memories away and looked around to see that everyone was gone from the gravesite, except Lucy. She stood there, staring at him. He watched as she took a deep breath and walked to stand in front of him. He gazed into her gorgeous face and swore he felt his heart stop. Just as it always seemed to do when she looked at him, or smiled at him. Something she wasn't doing now.

"Reid, you have to leave now. I don't want you here anymore."

"I want to stay while they—"

"No! You will not see my husband lowered into the ground. You don't deserve to be here. Not anymore."

"Lucy, please. He was my best friend."

"Get out of here before I have someone remove you," she said through clenched teeth.

Reid took a deep breath and gave her a terse nod. "I understand."

"Do you? I hope so, because you put him in

there." She pointed to the flower-covered casket.

He felt the blood drain from his face as he stared at her. He turned on his boot heel and stalked across the wet grass toward his truck. When he reached it, he wanted to look back but didn't. He climbed into his truck, and with wheels spinning on gravel, he tore out of the cemetery as if the hounds of hell were chasing him, and perhaps they were.

Chapter One

Three Years Later

Reid stared down at the headstone with *Ezekiel "Zeke" Albright* carved into the marble. Only the dates of his birth and death accompanied his name—nothing else. No statement of how great of a bull rider he'd been, how much he'd loved his wife, and friends—nothing. Reid wasn't sure what was appropriate to put on a headstone, but he thought something more should be on there for Zeke, to tell the world who he was.

He took his hat off, squatted down, and spun the brim of the hat in his hands. It was still hard to believe Zeke was gone. A tear rolled down his cheek.

"I miss you, buddy," he whispered.

He hadn't realized he wasn't alone until he looked over and saw jean-clad legs. His eyes traveled up them and he found himself staring at the one person he was hoping to avoid while he was home for the holidays. Lucy Albright. He came to his feet quickly and placed his hat on his head.

"Reid?" She frowned up at him.

He nodded. "I'm sorry. I'll leave, Lucy."

"No. Please stay."

Reid didn't move. They both stood there in silence for a few minutes, staring at the headstone.

"You were right," he whispered.

"About what?"

"It was my fault."

He heard her gasp and felt her hand on his arm, but he couldn't look at her. "No, Reid. It wasn't your fault. I know I blamed you at first, but Zeke made the decision to ride. You didn't make him do it."

"I tried to help him but I couldn't reach him when he put his hand out to me." He took a deep breath. "I couldn't reach him," he repeated.

"I was there too, Reid. I saw what happened. I know you tried. I saw Zeke reach out for you."

"I see him doing that in my dreams almost every night."

"I did for a long time. I blamed you for talking him into riding, and for not helping him."

Reid winced. "Not as much as I blamed myself."

"Reid, Zeke was his own man. He made the decision to ride. I begged him not to. He told me he wanted one more ride." She shook her head. "He got it."

"I should have done more to help him. When I first saw him in trouble, I wanted to jump in there but the other cowboys held me back. Because I didn't, you lost a husband and I lost my best friend. I'll miss him every day for the rest of my life. I see his terrified face every night when I close my eyes. I'll never forget the look on his face as he reached his hand out to me and I couldn't reach him." He felt another tear roll down his face. "I'm so sorry, Lucy."

She squeezed his arm. "You don't have anything to be sorry for, Reid. It wasn't your fault. I know that. I came to realize it a long time ago. I had to blame someone other than myself, and Zeke."

Reid looked at her. "You have no blame in this at all."

"I do," she whispered.

Reid watched a tear roll down her face and it about brought him to his knees. He reached out to her and pulled her into his arms. She wrapped her arms around his waist, resting her head against his shoulder, and cried. He was man enough to let his tears go too. She was tall for a woman, almost five ten, but he still towered over her at six five. After a few minutes, she raised her head and looked up at him. He gazed down into her beautiful face. She smiled at him.

"Thank you for that. I haven't cried over Zeke in years." She pulled away from him. "Sometimes tears help you feel better." She reached up and wiped a tear from his cheek. She cleared her throat and started to walk away from him, when she suddenly turned back to face him. "Are you home for Christmas?"

"Yes. I was on my way to Mom and Dad's when I decided to stop here. I'm glad I did now. It's good to see you, Lucy. You look great." He smiled when a blush stained her cheeks. She was entirely too young to be a widow. Zeke had only been twenty-nine when he died. Too young.

"You look good too, Reid. I just wanted to stop by and put some flowers out for the holidays. I'm on my way home now. I hope you have a Merry Christmas, Reid."

"You too, Lucy." He gave her a nod and turned away from her. It about killed him to look at her. His best friend's wife was the one woman he'd always love, but could never have.

****

The next day, Lucy stood at the kitchen window staring out at the snow. Christmas was in four days. It seemed to come quicker every year. She lifted her cup to her lips to take a sip of her coffee.

"Mama?"

"In here, baby." She set her cup down and turned just in time to catch Zeke as he launched himself at her. She rubbed her cheek against his blond hair. He reminded her so much of his father. She missed that man so much. She missed his smile, and his kisses. The way he'd loved her, although she guessed he hadn't loved her enough to quit the rodeo circuit. Nothing could keep him from that one last ride. Sighing, she kissed Zeke's little fat cheek and set him down.

"Are you hungry?"

"Yep. I want mac cheese," Zeke told her. He always wanted mac and cheese.

"Sounds good. Go wash your hands and I'll get it ready for you." She laughed as he ran off.

Her smile faded as she thought of her son never knowing his father. She had no doubt that Zeke would've loved his little boy. She only wished he'd had the chance to meet him. She'd been devastated when Zeke died, and then she'd lashed out at Reid. When she thought back to the day of the funeral, she cringed. The things she'd said to him were unforgivable. Later, she'd read that he had retired from the rodeo at the height of his career. He went out a champion, and he deserved an apology for the appalling way

13

she'd treated him.

The ding of the microwave brought her back to the present. Zeke ran into the kitchen and pushed his chair out from the table.

"Lift me, Mama." He giggled raising his arms in the air.

Lucy smiled and lifted him into his booster seat. She placed the bowl of mac and cheese in front of him.

"Be careful, it's hot. Blow on it."

Zeke grinned, lifted his spoon, and blew on the mac and cheese too hard and some of it fell onto the table. He giggled as he picked it up and shoved it into his mouth. Lucy shook her head.

"Zeke, you are a silly boy," she said, but laughed when he turned a big smile her way. "Eat up. We need to go shopping for Nana and Pap."

"Yep. I know what to get Nana. A big ring. Just like the ones she wears."

Lucy bit back a laugh. The rings her mother wore were big diamonds and the thought of Zeke buying her one was laughable, but it would be fun watching him find one for her. She pulled out a chair and took a seat to eat her salad.

"Santa will be here soon, Mama. I've been a good boy, haven't I?"

"Of course you have, baby. Santa will be good to you."

"Do you think he'll bring me a pony like I want?"

"You'll just have to wait and see." Lucy smiled.

"I really want a pony." Zeke frowned.

"I know you do, and Santa does his best to get all little boys and girls what they ask for but sometimes, he just can't do it. So don't be disappointed if you don't get a pony, okay?"

Zeke shook his head. "Mama, I want a pony bad."

"I know you do but you'll get other nice presents too. Maybe Santa will bring you that bike you want so much."

Zeke nodded as he shoveled food into his mouth. "Yeah, that would be good too...not as good as a pony, but good. I told him I wanted a pony more than anything." After he finished eating, he pushed away from the table. "I'm done."

"Okay, go wash your face and then we'll leave." She smiled at his excitement when he ran off. Of course, it was hardly a minute later before he came rushing back into the kitchen.

"You missed a spot. Come here," she said. He ran to stand in front of her. He never seemed to walk anywhere. She wiped his face with a wet paper towel. "Get your coat, hat, and gloves. I'll go warm up the car."

"Okie dokie."

Lucy picked up the keys to her SUV and ran out to the vehicle. The cold snatched away her breath. Flurries swirled around her. No accumulation yet, but the weather station was calling for up to a foot of snow. She opened the door and climbed inside. She started the vehicle, turned the defroster and heat on, and then headed back inside. Zeke stood waiting for her in the kitchen with his coat, hat, and mittens on. His boots were on the wrong feet which wasn't unusual, but he tried. Lucy kneeled down in front of him.

"Sit down, baby. You have your boots on wrong."

Zeke frowned up at her. "Okay," he said plopping down on the floor.

Lucy pulled his little cowboy boots off and put them on the correct feet. She helped him up, and he immediately started jumping up and down. She wished she had half his energy.

Lucy put her coat, hat, and gloves on then took his little hand in hers. They walked outside to the SUV. She buckled him into his car seat and climbed behind the wheel. She looked into the rearview mirror and smiled. He was the sweetest boy and she loved him so much. He had his daddy's blond hair and her light blue eyes. He was going to be a heartbreaker when he grew up.

She put the vehicle in drive and headed to town.

****

Reid entered the store and saw nothing but frenzied chaos in front of him. Damn, he hated Christmas shopping. Of course, it was no one's fault but his own for waiting so long to pick out gifts. He didn't come home for the holidays often, but this year he'd wanted to be there. The town of Spring City, Montana was small. Under a thousand people lived here, and by the looks of it, all of them were in Walton's Department store. He swore under his breath as he maneuvered his way through the crowd.

Why did everyone wait until the last minute? *You waited until the last minute.*

"Yeah, but I'm an idiot," Reid muttered aloud.

"What was that, hon?" An elderly woman

looked up at him.

He smiled. "Just talking to myself."

She chuckled. "Well, we all do that, and at this time of the year, I find myself doing it more than ever."

Reid grinned. "I do, too." He put his fingers to the brim of his Stetson and moved past her.

He had no idea what he was even looking for. What do you buy a woman who has everything? He sighed when he reached the women's department and stared at the selection of clothing. A robe would be nice. Did she need one? Hell if he knew. He exhaled as he stepped to the rack lined with robes. What size? *Jesus! Shouldn't you have thought of this before you came here?*

He browsed through the rack moving each one past after deciding it was one that she wouldn't like. Her favorite color was pink; he knew that much. He pulled one off the rack and held it up. It was pink velour with a zipper up the front. The pull-tab had a pink ribbon attached to it for easy zipping, he supposed. She might like this, he thought.

"You look like you're concentrating awfully hard on that robe," a female voice said from beside him. Reid glanced over to see a very pretty woman with blonde hair smiling at him. He grinned at her.

"I don't like Christmas shopping," he told her.

She laughed. "Most men don't. Do you need some help?"

"Do you work here?"

"No. Just asking." She smiled at him again. He knew she was flirting and he didn't see anything wrong with that because she was very pretty.

"I just don't know..." He stopped when he spotted Lucy walking past in the aisle. She was looking down at something alongside her and smiling. When she glanced up, her eyes connected with his. She stopped in her tracks and her face turned pink. He saw her swallow hard then take a deep breath before walking toward him. The closer she got, the harder his heart pounded. She was so beautiful. He couldn't take his eyes off her face. She stopped in front of him and looked up at him.

"Hello, Lucy," he said in a rough voice then cleared his throat. She'd always had this kind of effect on him.

"Hey Reid. Are you getting your shopping done?"

"I'm trying. What are you—" His words caught in his throat when he glanced down and saw the little blond-haired boy holding her hand. He looked back to Lucy. "Is he...?"

"Yes. I was pregnant when Zeke died. He just turned three in September."

"I'm sorry. I didn't know."

"I'm the only who knew at the funeral." She looked at the robe in his hand, and then to the woman standing beside him. "I'll let you both get on with your shopping."

Reid glanced to the woman beside him and back to Lucy. "Uh, no...we're not together. I was just looking for something for someone, and she was helping me."

"I can see you don't need my help any longer," the blonde said before walking away.

Reid nodded but didn't take his eyes off the

little boy. "He looks just like Zeke." His voice caught and he swallowed hard.

"Yes, he does." Lucy squatted down. "Zeke, this is Reid Callahan, an old friend of...mine."

"Hello, Zeke," Reid said, putting his hand out to the little boy.

"Hello," Zeke said, as he placed his little hand in Reid's much larger one.

Reid swallowed hard again, and quickly blinked tears away. Zeke's son looked so much like him it was scary. Reid glanced away and took a deep breath. He looked back to Lucy.

"Are you shopping too?"

"Zeke and I have some things to get for Christmas. He's going to buy his nana a diamond ring." She winked.

"Wow. That's great." Reid squatted down so he was face to face with Zeke. "Does your nana like diamond rings, Z-man?"

Zeke's eyes lit up at the nickname. He gazed up at Lucy. "He called me Z-man, Mama."

Lucy laughed. "I heard that. Do you like that?"

"Yep."

Reid laughed. "A simple yep is good."

"It's his favorite word...that, and of course, no." Lucy glanced at the robe in his hands. "Is that the one you're getting?"

Reid stood. "I think so. She loves pink, but I'm not sure of the size."

"You're not sure of your wife's size?"

"Wife?" Reid frowned then realization dawned on him. "Oh, no...this is for my mom."

"Oh well then, I'd say your mom is about a size ten."

"Okay." Reid looked at the label on the robe. It

19

was a twelve. He put it back and found an identical robe in a size ten. He turned to look at Zeke. "So, Z-man, are you ready for Santa?"

"Yep. I want a pony this year. Mama says my daddy rode ponies when he was little, so I want to be like him."

Reid noticed Lucy blink her eyes quickly. He knew how she felt because he had a lump in his throat too.

"Your daddy was a great guy."

"Did you know my daddy? I didn't know him. He died before I was borned."

"I knew him very well."

"Reid was your daddy's best friend, baby. They did everything together. Reid misses him too."

Reid stared at her in wonder.

"Reid, I'm so sorry for what I said to you at the funeral. It was wrong."

"It's all right, Lucy."

"No. It's not. I'd love to make it up to you, how about coming over for dinner tonight. Unless you have to be at your mom's?"

"I'd...I'd love that. What time?"

"Six? We still live on the ranch."

"Six is fine. I'll see you then. I need to get going. I have to get something for my dad yet. I'll see you tonight then. See ya, Z-man." Reid grinned at them.

"Bye, Reid." Zeke pronounced his name as *Weid* and waved at him as Lucy led him away. Reid couldn't take his eyes off her.

****

Lucy stopped in the men's wear department then watched Reid stride away, and couldn't stop her eyes from going to his ass in those jeans of his. The man always could fill out a pair of jeans. She'd done everything she could to keep her eyes off the rodeo buckle he wore. It was way too close to the fly of his jeans.

She'd always thought Reid Callahan was one incredibly good-looking man. He stood six foot five, had black hair, and beautiful gray eyes. His nose was straight and sat above a kissable set of lips, although she'd never had a chance to kiss them. Even though he was clean-shaven, his lower face, neck, and jaw sported a faint shadow. She'd known the reputation he had while on the circuit, and wondered if he had someone special now.

Her insides shivered thinking back to that time. She'd hated the sport even though she'd met Zeke at a rodeo. She'd been only eighteen, seven years ago when she'd met the twenty-five year old Zeke Albright. Had he lived, he'd be thirty-two now and still in the prime of his life. She'd been so infatuated with him from the first moment they'd met. A friend had invited her to the rodeo and she felt mesmerized by all the sexy cowboys there. On her way to the concession stand to get popcorn, she'd literally run into Zeke almost knocking him down. He stood only a few inches taller than she did but he seemed larger than life. He'd laughed at her and asked her to go for a burger with him after the events. She agreed, but only if her friend went along. He was fine with that. They'd started dating, and she soon fell madly in love with him. They married a year after meeting, but they also fought constantly about him riding. It terrified her that he'd be hurt, or worse, killed. Her fears had come true.

She'd been so in love with Zeke that she hadn't paid much attention to Reid until one night, about a month after her wedding, when she was at a rodeo with Zeke she'd seen him talking with a woman and smiling at her like she was the only woman in the arena. The young woman stood with her back against a wall and Reid stood close with his hand placed above her head. Lucy realized just how devastatingly handsome he was, and felt so guilty about having even thought that way about him after that, she gave him the cold shoulder any time she was around him. As if was his fault she was attracted to him. She loved Zeke, she never doubted that ever, but sometimes looking at Reid made her wish she'd met him first.

She shook her head at the memories. Zeke had loved her and she would never have hurt him. Zeke had never known how she felt about Reid, and she supposed that since she'd never acted on her attraction, there had never been a reason to tell him. Seeing Reid today only intensified her feelings. If it was possible, he was even better looking than he was years ago. Now, she'd gone off the deep end and invited him to dinner tonight.

"What is wrong with you," she muttered under her breath.

"Nuttin', Mama. Why?"

"Not you, baby. I'm just thinking out loud."

"Okay. We need to see the rings now." Zeke tugged on her hand and led her toward the jewelry department. She spotted the costume jewelry and turned him in that direction. With her luck, he'd spot a real diamond and want to buy that for his nana.

"Okay, little man, here we are." She scooped him up into her arms so he could see all the goodies on display.

"You can call me Z-man, Mama," he said with a proud grin.

Lucy did her best not to laugh. "All right, Z-man. See if you can find something nice here."

Zeke looked at the jewelry with a frown on his face. He concentrated on each ring he saw. Finally, he picked one up.

"This one, Mama. Do you think Nana will like it?"

Lucy took the ring from him and smiled. "Of course, she will."

It was a huge cluster of fake diamonds with a silver band. It looked just like the kind of real ring her mother would buy. She did love her diamonds and Lucy knew she'd love this one just as much as a real one.

"Now, I have to get Pap something." Zeke scrunched up his nose. "Pap is hard to buy for."

"You're right about that. Let's look at some flannel shirts. He could always use one of those."

"Okay," Zeke said as he started hopping from one foot to the other with excitement. He stopped and stared up at her. "Mama? Is Reid gonna have supper with us?"

"Yes, he is. Why?"

"Just wondering. I like him. Is he a real cowboy?"

"Yes. He used to be on the rodeo circuit."

"What's a circuit?"

"Different types of events in different arenas,

like the rodeo."

Zeke nodded. "Can he ride a horse?"

"Yes, baby, yes, he can."

In her mind's eye, Lucy could see Reid sitting astride a horse. He used to compete in so many events. She'd loved watching him barrel race. He'd been fantastic at it, he'd have that horse so close to the ground going around those barrels that it looked as if the horse were on its side, but she knew his first love was riding the bulls. Just like Zeke. She quit watching the rodeo three years ago. He'd made a lot of money while bull riding and he'd been champion two years in a row before Zeke died, and one year after that. Buckle bunnies always surrounded him. Zeke had his share too, until he married her anyway, and she began to travel with him for every show.

They'd purchased the ranch a year before he died. Zeke had paid cash for it, and with the life insurance he'd taken out, she was set for life. She loved the ranch. It was just hard taking care of it with only her and one ranch hand. She knew she'd have to hire at least one more man in the near future. The horses were a handful for just two people. She raised Paints with a great bloodline. They were her favorite breed of horse. Zeke had bought her one for their first anniversary, and she knew then what she wanted to do. The only real competition she had was from Ryder Wolfe in nearby Clifton.

Zeke had helped her get customers from his rodeo friends. Her business took off like wildfire but when Zeke died, she'd almost quit. She'd wanted to sell the ranch and disappear. The pain she'd felt over losing her husband had almost done her in. There were nights, however, when she'd lay in bed and wonder if they'd still be together. Her infatuation with Reid would have grown stronger because she would have seen him more often. *God!* He was still so tempting and sexy. He was the same age as Zeke, but just seemed like so much more a *man.* Damn, he was still single and still smoking hot.

Lucy sighed. It didn't matter though because she would never get involved with any man who competed in bull riding, ever again. Even though he'd supposedly retired, the pull of the rodeo would always be there—a temptation hard to resist. *So, why invite him to dinner?* She shook her head...because she was an idiot.

Chapter Two

Reid pulled into the driveway of the Rolling A ranch. He remembered the day Zeke first told him about it. *It's perfect, man. Luce and I are going to raise our children there and grow old together. I'm going to have a house built with a huge front porch with rocking chairs on it. We'll sit there and watch the kids play in the front yard.*

Reid cleared his throat as he pulled his truck up to the front of the house. It was just as Zeke had wanted it to be. A porch stretched across the entire front of the log home. A porch, Zeke would never sit on watching his son run around the yard or ride a pony. *Damn it!* Why was life so cruel? Zeke should still be here with his wife and son. Taking a deep breath, Reid stepped from the truck and walked up the steps to the front door. He rang the doorbell and waited.

Lucy opened the door and stood there smiling at him. "Come in. You're just in time."

Reid wiped his feet on the mat, taking his hat off as he entered the house. He'd been here many times, but this visit made him feel very uncomfortable. He glanced around as he entered. It was still the same. A large living room sat to his right. A fire roared in the stone fireplace, and the house smelled of fresh pine due to the large Christmas tree in the corner with its twinkling lights. Two stockings hung from the mantle where three should have been.

A large overstuffed sofa faced the fireplace. A large flat-screen TV hung above the mantle, and two chairs bracketed the sofa. Scattered rugs covered the dark oak hardwood floors. A dark cherry rocking chair sat by the large front window. Reid stared at the room as if seeing it for the first time.

"Are you all right, Reid?" Lucy asked him gently touching his arm.

"Uh, yeah...I'm fine." He smiled at her.

"Take a seat. Dinner will be ready in just a few minutes. I made spaghetti. Its Zeke's favorite. That and mac and cheese." She laughed.

"I love spaghetti. Sounds great." Reid hesitantly moved into the living room.

"Oh hey, let me have your coat, Reid," Lucy exclaimed from beside him. He took it off and handed it to her.

Zeke came running into the room and jumped onto the sofa.

"Hi, Reid." The boy, who reminded him so much of his best friend, smiled up at him.

"Hey, Z-man...what's going on?"

"Nuttin'. We're having p'sgetti for supper."

Reid grinned. "I know. I love p'sgetti. How about you?"

Zeke fell back on the couch and giggled. "You said it wrong."

Reid frowned. "I did? That's how you said it."

"Yep, but I'm a little boy," Zeke said with grown up knowledge.

"I see." Reid ran his hand over his mouth to hide a grin.

"Mama said you're a real cowboy." Zeke got to his knees, leaned on the arm of the sofa and stared at him.

"Yes, sir. I most certainly am. I have the hat to

prove it." Reid pointed to his hat that he'd perched on his bent knee.

"I have a cowboy hat too. I'll go get it."

He hopped down from the sofa and ran off down the hallway. A few minutes later, he returned with a black Stetson perched on his head. It was too big and Reid knew why. It had belonged to Zeke. Reid swallowed past the lump in his throat. Damn it, this was so hard.

"That's some hat, cowboy."

"It was my daddy's. Mama said he always wore it."

"Yes, he did."

"My head will grow one day and it will fit me."

Reid couldn't help it, he laughed. "Yes."

Lucy entered the room and stared at Zeke. "Are you bothering Reid?"

"Nope. He said I was a cowboy too."

"I'm sorry…" Reid hadn't wanted to stir up bad memories.

"Its fine, Reid, I call him cowboy all the time. You don't have to tiptoe around me about Zeke. He's been gone over three years now. I'll always love him, but I've moved on. Come on, dinner is ready."

Reid watched her walk away. *Moved on? What the hell did that mean? Did she have a man in her life now?*

Damn, the thought hit him like a ton of bricks. He stood and followed them to the kitchen. Nothing had changed in that room either. The large window above the sink still had hanging baskets with plants in front of it. The large butcher-block table sat centered on a braided rug. He watched as Lucy placed the spaghetti on the table, along with garlic bread. The room smelled wonderful and in reaction, his stomach rumbled.

"Hungry, are you?" Lucy laughed.

Reid grinned. "Starving."

"Sit. Please."

"I will, after you do."

Lucy smiled at him and his heart hit his stomach. She put Zeke in his booster seat then pulled out a chair and sat down. Reid sat after she did.

"Your mom raised you right, Reid."

"Did you raise me right, Mama?"

"I like to think so, Zeke."

"Z-man, Mama."

Lucy tipped her head down and Reid knew it was to hide a smile. "Yes, sir. I forgot." She raised her eyes and looked at Reid. Her smile seemed to fade when their eyes met and held.

Reid glanced away. *You can't be lusting after your best friend's wife. It wasn't right then and sure as hell isn't right now.* He mentally shook his head and looked at Zeke.

"Tell me what you want for Christmas, besides a pony, Z-man." Reid waited until Lucy put spaghetti on hers and Zeke's plates before piling some onto his own, and then took a slice of garlic bread.

Rcid and Lucy listened as Zeke rattled off a list of toys. Reid raised an eyebrow at Lucy. She shrugged and dug into her spaghetti.

****

Oh, this was a bad, bad idea, Lucy Albright!

She chastised herself for even thinking she could just be friends with Reid. The spaghetti had no taste whatsoever, but she continued to eat. She listened to Reid and Zeke talking. Reid would laugh when Zeke told one of his jokes. Jokes that never made sense but would make him giggle uncontrollably. She suppressed a tremor of heated desire when Reid's deep chuckle moved over her. *Shit!* He was so sexy. She quickly glanced up when she heard Reid say her name. She saw a frown on his face, which made her think he'd spoken her name more than once. She could feel the heat pour into her cheeks.

"I'm sorry. I was thinking of...something."

"I was just saying the spaghetti is great." Reid smiled at her.

Suddenly, she couldn't stop looking at the deep creases in his cheeks. *Dimples.* She'd always been a sucker for a man with dimples, but were his always so sexy. Fine lines fanned out from his eyes. Thick lashes surrounded those beautiful gray eyes and she wanted to smack him for having longer lashes than she did. *How was that fair?*

"Thank you. It's my mom's recipe," Lucy said poking at her food with her fork.

"Nana makes good p'sgetti too. I like mac cheese. Do you like mac cheese, Reid?" Zeke asked wiping a messy hand across his mouth.

"As a matter of fact, I do." Reid winked at Lucy and she almost fell out of her chair.

Good heavens, Lucy Albright! You'd think a man never winked at you before. You're getting hot over a man talking about mac and cheese. Horny. She realized she was horny! She groaned and almost died of embarrassment when Reid frowned at her.

"Are you all right?"

"Yes, of course. I just love spaghetti." Lucy knew she was blushing and was hoping a hole would open under her and swallow her up. *Now. Now, would be good.* She inwardly sighed...no such luck.

"O-kay," Reid said as he continued to frown at her. When she narrowed her eyes at him, he looked down and then picked up his water, and took a drink.

"If Santa brings me a pony, how will it fit down the chimley?"

Reid started choking on his water. Lucy stood up and smacked him on the back. He looked up at her with tears in his eyes.

"You have to be prepared for anything with a three-year-old," Lucy said laughing.

Reid shook his head, and coughed. "I wasn't ready for that."

Zeke frowned at both adults. "Did it go down wrong, Reid?"

Reid burst out laughing. "Yeah, Z-man, it did."

After dinner, Lucy told them to go to the living room while she cleaned up. Reid left the kitchen with Zeke. Lucy muttered under her breath when they disappeared. She needed some heavenly help to get her through the rest of the evening. When Reid laughed earlier, she couldn't keep her eyes from his gorgeous smile. His teeth were white, straight, and perfect. The man had it all.

She loaded the dishwasher, wiped off the stove, and then leaned against the counter. Now what was she to do? She could hear Reid's deep voice as he talked with Zeke. She smiled when she heard Zeke giggle. He seemed to like Reid a lot. Lucy frowned. That could be a very bad thing because Reid would be leaving so she didn't want Zeke to get too attached. She was sure he'd be leaving after the holidays.

Taking a deep breath, she pushed away from the counter and headed for the living room. She stopped in the doorway and smiled when she saw them sitting on the couch together. Reid glanced up at her and smiled. Her heart slammed against her ribs.

"What's going on with you two," she asked, suddenly suspicious at how behaved her little boy was being.

"We can't tell you, Mama. It's about Christmas presents." Zeke put his hands over his mouth as he giggled.

"Yeah, we can't tell you," Reid added with a grin.

Lucy smiled without thinking as she entered the living room and sat in one of the chairs. She picked up the remote and turned the TV on. Zeke scrambled to his knees.

"Find me a Christmas movie, Mama. Please."

"I'm looking." Lucy clicked the remote until she saw one he loved. "How about *The Santa Clause*?"

Zeke jumped off the couch and clapped his hands. "Yes, please." He turned to face Reid. "You have to stay and watch it with me."

"Uh..."

"Please," Zeke begged.

"Baby, Reid may need to get home." Lucy looked at Reid. "You don't have to stay."

"I don't mind, if you don't."

"No. We'd love to have you stay."

Reid nodded. "I will then. Thanks."

They all relaxed and watched the movie. Before it was over, Zeke was sound asleep on the couch with his head in Reid's lap. Lucy blinked tears back from her eyes. He needed a father in his life. She stood and moved to the couch.

"I'll put him to bed and be right back," she whispered.

Reid nodded. "Do you need me to carry him?"

She shook her head, picked Zeke up, and carried him down the hallway to his bedroom.

****

Reid sat forward and drew his hands down his face. He needed a kick in the ass for agreeing to stay for the movie. He had to get the hell out of here. As soon as Lucy came back, he was gone. He was already beginning to like Zeke too much, and he knew he shouldn't. He was going back home to Butte after New Year's Day. It was for the best. Lucy would never feel about him the way he felt about her. She'd already had the love of her life, and Reid hated being second in anything. He stood when she entered the room.

"He didn't even stir when I changed him into his pajamas," she said as she leaned against the doorjamb.

"I wish I could sleep like that," Reid muttered.

"Me too." She crossed her arms and Reid's eyes strayed to her breasts.

"I'd better go. Thank you for dinner. It was very good."

"You're welcome. I wanted to make it up to you for the way I had treated you."

"I deserved it, Lucy."

"No, you did not, Reid Callahan."

"He's why you blame yourself, isn't he?" Reid jerked his chin toward the hallway.

"Yes. I can't help but think that had I told Zeke I was pregnant, he might've stayed home. I had just taken a pregnancy test a few days before he told me he wanted to go. I knew if I'd told him and he stayed home because of me, he'd resent me for it. But then again, if I'd told him, he might still be alive."

Reid shook his head at her thinking. "I seriously doubt that, Lucy. He would have gone just so he could brag that you were carrying his baby."

Lucy chuckled. "You could be right, that would be like Zeke."

"I know I'm right. He loved talking about you to anyone who would listen." Reid stared at her and then walked toward her. He stopped beside her in the doorway of the living room. "I hope you have a Merry Christmas." He tilted his head. "I'm curious. Is Santa bringing Z-man a pony?"

Lucy laughed. "Of course. I've done everything to give him the impression that Santa can't bring everything we ask for, but he won't believe that."

Reid grinned. "Smart boy." He glanced up and saw mistletoe hanging above him. He looked at Lucy. "Tradition," he murmured as he leaned toward her.

She straightened up and he was sure she was going to tell him not to do it but when she didn't, he lightly kissed her lips. He was sure his heart skipped a beat. Her hands went to his shoulders and his wrapped around her waist. He pressed his lips to hers again and groaned against them.

When she moaned and opened to him, he moved his tongue into her mouth. He pulled her tighter against him and he knew she had to feel his hard cock pressing against the fly of his jeans. He slowly raised his head and stared into her beautiful blue eyes.

"I'm sorry..."

"Jesus, Reid. Stop apologizing. I was right there with you."

"I need to get going. Could you get my coat?"

Lucy looked like she was going to argue but then she spun on her heel, and walked down the hallway. She returned in less than a minute with his sheepskin coat. She handed it to him. He shrugged into it and placed his hat on his head.

"Goodnight. Merry Christmas," he said, as he walked out the door, and climbed into his truck. He slammed his hand against the steering wheel.

"You're a fucking idiot," he said aloud to the empty cab. "What in the hell were you thinking? Stupid son of a bitch," he muttered, turning the ignition over.

Reid drove home to his parents' house where he pulled up to the back of the two-story white farmhouse, stopped and shut the truck off. He wrapped his hands around the steering wheel as he tried to calm himself. Her lips were softer than he'd ever imagined. He wanted her—so much. He had for years.

Shaking his head, he climbed out of the truck and entered the dark kitchen. He could hear the TV in the living room and headed that way. His dad sat in the recliner with his feet up, watching an old movie.

"Hey, Dad," Reid said quietly as he removed

his hat and coat. He laid his coat over the back of the other recliner.

His dad looked up at him and smiled. "Hey, son. Did you have a date," his dad asked with a slight Irish brogue.

"No. Actually, I had dinner with Lucy Albright and her son."

"No shit?"

Reid chuckled. "No shit."

Reid tossed his hat to the sofa and then walked around the recliner, and sat down. He pulled the lever to raise the footrest.

"How'd it go?"

"Good. Did you know she had a son?"

"Yeah. I've seen her in town."

"Why didn't you tell me?"

His dad looked over to him and frowned. "Reid, you've blamed yourself for Zeke's death for years. I knew if you found out he had a son, you'd never get past your guilt."

"It just floored me. He looks just like Zeke."

"He does. Acts like him too." His dad chuckled. "A little tornado is what he is."

"You're telling me. He talks a thousand miles an hour, just like Zeke used to. He loves telling jokes too. He asked me what the banana said, and when I asked what, he said because it's yellow."

His dad laughed. "So, how did you end up having dinner with the woman who cut you into pieces at the funeral?"

"She doesn't blame me anymore. We had a long talk. She's been blaming herself too, for a long time. She feels if she'd told him she was pregnant, he wouldn't have gone to that rodeo."

36

"Did you tell her that was bullshit?"

Reid laughed. Leave it to his dad just to tell it like was. Declan Callahan was never one to mince words.

"I did. She told me she originally blamed me because she didn't want to blame Zeke but in the end, he was man enough to make his own decisions."

"She's right, son. No one twisted Zeke's arm. He made up his own mind. It was a damn shame what happened but the only person responsible for going or not going, was Zeke." Declan sighed. "I know you miss him. He was your best friend, but you can't keep blaming yourself for something you had no control over."

"I know, Dad," Reid said in a low voice.

"Does she know how you feel about her?"

Reid was startled. "What?"

"You might be able to hide it from others, but your mom and I have always known."

"How?"

"We saw the way you looked at her at their wedding reception."

"Shit," Reid murmured.

"Don't worry. I don't think anyone else noticed. They were too involved watching Lucy and Zeke."

"She'll never know. She was married to my best friend."

"And he's gone." Declan put his hand up when Reid started to interrupt. "Life goes on, Reid. Who knows? Maybe she's the one for you."

Reid had no comment. That kiss came rushing back into his mind. It had felt so right, but how did she feel about it? She didn't push him away or tell him no. She'd wrapped her arms around him and held him tight. *Shit! Shit! Shit!* She'd been married to Zeke for three years. Reid knew she loved Zeke more than anyone was able. Her heart broke when he died. Reid would never forget seeing her in pain at the funeral. He hadn't gone to the funeral home. He couldn't stomach seeing Zeke lain out in that casket. It was hard enough just knowing he was inside it at the cemetery.

"I don't think so, Dad. She loved Zeke so much. I don't think any man could live up to that."

"You don't have to live up to him. She doesn't want another Zeke. She needs someone completely new for her. She works hard on that ranch of hers and she only has one ranch hand." Declan shrugged. "If you decide to stick around, maybe you could help out a little. Just sayin'..."

"You're incorrigible," Reid said, laughing.

Declan chuckled. "Maybe. But I'd like to see my son happy, and you haven't been since Zeke died."

"I'll get there eventually."

"Oh hey, by the way, could you pick up a Christmas tree for us tomorrow? I haven't had a chance yet."

"Sure, Dad, I'll get one tomorrow."

"I believe you got one four years ago on the Rolling A, didn't you?"

"Damn, Dad. Quit playing matchmaker. I'll get me a woman one day."

"Please do before your dad and I are too old to enjoy our grandchildren," Catherina Callahan said as she stepped into the room.

"Aw, Mom, not you too," Reid muttered.

She laughed, and coming to stand alongside his chair, she placed her hand on his head. "Sorry, honey. Come on, Declan, before you fall asleep in your chair."

"I never fall asleep in my chair, Cat. Where did you ever get an idea like that?" Declan winked at Reid as he let the footrest down on the recliner and stood. "Goodnight son, sleep well, for once."

Catherina leaned down and kissed the top of Reid's head. "Goodnight, Reid. I agree with your dad. Sleep well, honey."

"Goodnight Mom. Dad. I'll see you in the morning."

"Don't forget to get a tree," Declan called out as he put his arm around Catherina and they disappeared up the stairs.

Reid chuckled. His dad was such a character. Reid knew his parents wanted him to be happy and he hadn't been in over three years. Lucy's heart wasn't the only one that broke when Zeke died. He wanted to crawl inside the casket with him, as morbid as that sounded. They'd become friends in the second grade and remained inseparable ever since...until he died anyway. After graduation, they'd headed to Oklahoma together to learn how to ride the bulls. They hit the rodeo circuit in their early twenties and in no time were at the top. They loved the competition between each other but were happy when the other won. Zeke would have been so proud of Reid winning again for the third time in his career.

Reid sighed and rubbed his jaw. Zeke wouldn't be happy with him kissing his wife though. Reid used to tease him that if he'd seen Lucy first, she'd belong to him. Only he knew that he hadn't been joking. It was wishful thinking but if it were possible to turn back time, he'd find her and make her his before Zeke had. He leaned back in the chair and stared at the TV. He chuckled when he saw what movie was playing. Jimmy Stewart ran down the street in the snow, waving at the buildings and calling out to them. *If only we were all allowed to see how different life could be by changing a few things*. He closed his eyes and relived that kiss. He could see tonight wasn't going to bring much sleep.

Chapter Three

Lucy sat at the kitchen table, drinking her coffee. Zeke was still sleeping. This was her alone time when the house was quiet because it was too early for him to be up. She touched her fingertips to her lips. Reid's kiss still seemed to linger there. Why had he kissed her? Oh, sure, there was mistletoe, but not everyone kissed under it. Some people ignored it. Tradition, he'd said.

God! The man could kiss. She was sure her toes had curled. No man had ever kissed her like that, not even Zeke. The kiss was simply all consuming. Her insides quivered just thinking about it. She pushed her chair back and stood.

Hearing a vehicle outside, she walked to the door and peered out. She saw Reid climbing out of his truck. His brown Stetson sat low on his forehead and he wore gloves, but his sheepskin coat hung open. She couldn't stop her eyes from traveling down his broad chest to his crotch. She groaned as she stared. The jeans were tight around his thick thighs, and they cupped his sex, leaving little to the imagination. What she'd felt against her last night, she'd thought very impressive.

When he started toward the steps, she opened the back door. He came to a halt and stared up at her. Snow flurries swirled around him.

"I was hoping you were up," he said.

"I've been up a while. What are you doing here?"

He bounded up the steps and stood in front of her. "Would you mind if I cut a tree on your property?"

"No, not at all. There are still some beautiful ones up there."

"Dad wants me to get a tree and he remembered that I'd gotten one here before..."

"Before Zeke died, I know. You can say it, Reid. I'm not going to fall into a heap at your feet and cry."

He huffed. "I just find it hard to talk about him."

"You can say anything you want about him. I'm fine with it. I don't blame you, Reid. I mean that."

"All right, thank you. Do you have a horse I can borrow?"

"I have twenty in the barn to choose from, but come in and get a cup of coffee. It's awfully cold."

Reid stepped inside and removed his hat, gloves, and coat. After stuffing his gloves in the pockets, he hung his coat on the back of the chair and set his cowboy hat on the seat of an empty chair. He pulled a chair out, but waited for Lucy to sit before he did. He picked up the mug she'd set in front of him and sipped his coffee.

"Do you mind if Zeke and I go with you?" she asked before taking a sip of her coffee.

"No. In fact, that would be great. I'm not sure I remember where we got the last tree."

She smiled. "I'll show you then."

"Hi, Reid," Zeke yelled suddenly appearing at the door before running into the kitchen.

"Hey, Z-man, did you sleep well?" Reid lifted

his cup to take a sip of the hot brew.

"Yep. Did you sleep here with Mama?" Zeke stood alongside the table by Reid bouncing up and down in his bunny slippers.

Reid inhaled and nearly choked on the coffee. His eyes narrowed at Lucy when she burst out laughing.

"I warned you." She smiled, shaking her head.

Reid's lips twitched as he tried not to laugh. "Yes, you did. I'm going to quit taking a drink of anything with him around.

Lucy chuckled. "Let's get you some breakfast, Z-man, and then we're going horseback riding to find Reid a tree."

Zeke's eyes widened. "Can I ride with you, Reid?"

Reid glanced up at her for permission, and she nodded.

"Of course you can, Zeke."

"Z-man," Zeke stated with a big grin.

"Yes, sir."

Zeke screwed up his face in concentration then he nodded. "I guess it's okay to call me Zeke. It is my name." He looked at Lucy. "Huh, Mama?"

Lucy rolled her lips in to keep the smile at bay. "Yes and a great name it is."

Zeke giggled. "Thanks, Mama."

Lucy looked at Reid and saw him staring at Zeke with such sadness that she had to blink quickly to dispel the tears forming. She lightly touched his arm. His eyes shifted to her.

"Are you all right?"

He nodded but didn't speak. She watched as he blinked his eyes quickly then he looked at her.

"He is so much like Zeke," he said, his voice raw with emotion.

"I know. It amazes me. He never knew his daddy but yet, he's so much like him at times."

"When he laughs..." Reid shook his head.

"I know," she whispered. "Some days it makes me smile, and on others, I feel like crying."

"Lucy..."

"Don't you dare say you're sorry one more time, Reid Callahan. We've been over this. I know he would have gone no matter how much I begged him not to."

"But if I hadn't suggested it..."

"I'm going to let you in on a little secret. I caught him looking at the event before you even told him about it." She was lying, but she had to get Reid to stop blaming himself. She'd come to terms with her blame in all this and he needed to also.

"Why do I get the feeling you're just telling me that to make me feel better?"

Lucy laughed. "You'll never know."

Reid chuckled and shook his head. "True."

"Mama?"

"Yes, baby?"

"Let's go get Reid a tree."

"Don't you want some cereal first?"

Zeke giggled and ran around the table to push his chair out. He looked up at Reid. "Can you put me in my chair, Reid? Mama don't like me climbing." He put his arms out toward Reid.

Reid looked startled but he picked Zeke up, put him in his booster seat, and snapped the seatbelt around him. Zeke grinned up at him. Lucy could see Reid was having trouble holding it together.

"Eat your breakfast, Zeke and then we'll go with Reid," she told her son.

Reid glanced away, and returned to his seat. Lucy refilled his coffee and set it in front of him. He glanced up at her with a smile.

"Thank you. It *is* cold out there, so you two will need to bundle up."

"Can I wear my cowboy hat like Reid?" Zeke picked up his spoon to begin eating.

"Your cowboy hat is too big to keep your head warm. You can wear your beanie," Lucy said.

"I don't like my beanie," Zeke announced with a frown.

"You'll wear it or I'll leave you here with RJ," Lucy told him.

"RJ?" Reid asked her with curiosity.

"My ranch hand. He loves watching Zeke for me when I have something to do."

"I see. Well, Z-man, you'd better make up your mind. I'll need help choosing a tree. I can't depend on your mom." Reid leaned toward Zeke and lowered his voice to a whisper. "She's a girl."

Zeke giggled. "Okay, I'll wear my beanie."

Lucy narrowed her eyes at Reid. "I'm a girl?"

She watched as he ran his eyes over her from the top of her head, on down to her feet. She could feel a blush staining her cheeks. He winked at her. "You sure are, darlin'."

He chuckled when she snorted and returned to her seat with a fresh cup of coffee.

****

Reid wasn't sure what had possessed him to call her darlin' and wink at her. Other than the fact, he couldn't help himself. He wanted her so much. He felt his dick trying to push against his zipper. *Down boy!* He quickly stood, making Zeke and Lucy stare up at him.

"I'll go saddle the horses. I'll be right back." He slammed his hat onto his head, pulled his coat off the back of the chair, and headed out the door pulling his gloves on as he went. Once he hit the porch and the cold air blew around him, his dick finally listened. *Shit!*

This was such a bad idea. He pulled his coat on. Zeke was one adorable little boy and he reminded Reid so much of his daddy. The only thing was he had Lucy's blue eyes, not his father's hazel ones. As for Lucy...well, he'd always loved her.

He was leaving after the holidays so no good could come from this but damn, he didn't want to stay away from them. He walked down the steps and headed for the barn. Once inside, he let his eyes adjust before walking down the center aisle. He stopped when he saw a young man walking toward him.

"Can I help you?" The man stopped and rested his fists at his hips.

"Are you RJ?" Reid asked with a tentative smile.

"Yes sir and you are?"

"Reid Callahan." Reid stuck his hand out.

"You're Reid Callahan? The bull rider?"

Reid nodded with more than a bit of self-conscious embarrassment. "Yes."

"Damn," RJ said and grabbed Reid's hand to shake it. "I saw you ride about two years ago."

"I won that year."

"I know. Man, I'd love your autograph."

"I don't have any photos with me but I'll get you one, and bring it back. Will that work?"

"Oh, yes sir." RJ kept staring at him, and then he frowned. "But, why are you here?"

"I'm friends with Lucy. Her husband and I were best friends."

RJ nodded. "Real shame about him, I remember now. You were there when it happened. Man, I remember you trying to get to him."

Reid nodded wanting to change the subject. "I need to saddle two horses. Lucy is taking me up to the north pasture to cut a tree."

"All right then, I'll help you. Come with me. Lucy has some great horses. Is Zeke going?"

"Yes, he's going to ride with me."

Reid followed him through the barn to the horses. He admired the horseflesh Lucy owned. She loved her Paints. He listened to RJ ramble on as he got saddles and blankets for the horses. It made him wonder about RJ. He didn't seem very old. Was Lucy involved with the good-looking ranch hand? Reid ran his eyes over him. He was tall, close to six-foot, blond hair and blue eyes. He just seemed so young. More like a kid than a man.

"How long have you worked here, RJ?"

"Three years now. Lucy hired me right out of high school. I needed a job, so she was nice enough to give me one."

High school? So the kid *was* a kid. He couldn't be more than twenty-one. Maybe Lucy liked younger men. She was only twenty-five after all, just four years older than RJ. *Damn!* Reid muttered under his breath. He had no right to be jealous of this...kid. Lucy was just now starting to accept Reid as a friend. He shook his head at that idea. A friend was the last thing he wanted to be to her. And since kissing her...well, what he wanted made him an idiot. He watched RJ lead two horses toward him. One was a black and white tall horse, the other a shorter, brown, and white beauty.

"I saddled Acer for you, since you're so tall. This one is Lucy's horse. Her name is Dixie."

"Thanks, I appreciate it," Reid said as he took the reins from him and led the horses from the barn. He saw Lucy and Zeke standing on the porch. Well, Lucy was standing; Zeke was jumping up and down. Reid laughed at the little boy.

"Does he ever stay still?"

"Yes...when he's sleeping." Lucy smiled at him and his heart jumped in his chest.

"You have some beautiful horses, Lucy."

"I see that RJ saddled Acer for you. He's a big horse. Just what you need."

What he needed was to have her under him or above him. *Fuck! Here we go again.* He smiled and hoped like hell, she didn't notice that he had a hard-on. He turned to face the horse.

"Do you need a leg up," he asked over the neck of the horse.

"Excuse me? I've been riding for years."

Reid smiled. "Just checking."

"You get up first, and I'll hand Zeke up to you."

"Z-man, Mama," Zeke corrected her.

"Sorry, baby. Come here and let me lift you up to Reid."

Reid vaulted onto the saddle and leaned down

48

to take Zeke from her. He set the boy in front of him on the saddle. "Ready, Z-man?'

"Yep." Zeke leaned his head back and stared up at him. "I think I like Z-man best."

Reid laughed, and then sobered when he saw Lucy pull herself up into the saddle. Her jeans stretched tight across her ass. He muttered under his breath as he felt his dick twitch again. He nudged the horse into a walk. He glanced over his shoulder to see Lucy coming up behind him.

"The trees are beautiful up there. I'm sure you'll be able to find one. Did you bring an axe?"

"Yes, ma'am."

Zeke sat in front of him trying to catch snowflakes on his tongue. He turned his head and looked at Reid.

"Can we build a snowman?"

"I don't see why not, but let me find a tree first."

"Okie dokie. Mama? Reid said we could build a snowman after he finds a tree."

"That will be fun, baby." Lucy leaned down and unhooked the chain on the fence that led to the pasture. She sat on her horse and waited for Reid to ride through before she followed.

****

Lucy watched Reid ride through, and then couldn't keep her eyes from staying on his broad back. The man knew how to sit a horse. He was all cowboy and sexy as hell. *Stay away from him and do not let him kiss you again!* She mentally groaned. She couldn't get that kiss out of her head. No man made her tingle all over like Reid had and that seemed so wrong. She had loved Zeke, but he'd never made her feel like that.

49

Ever. Why did that feel so wrong?

She blew out a breath and watched it form into a puff of cold air in front of her. It was damn cold out. She pulled the collar up on her coat and her beanie down over her ears. A cowboy hat didn't keep your ears warm. She stared up ahead at Reid's back. His hat sat down low and his collar was up, but she'd noticed when he rode through the gate, that his coat was open and he had it wrapped around Zeke. She smiled as she listened to Zeke chattering away and every once in a while she'd hear Reid's deep voice answering him but most of the time, he'd just nod. She knew how talkative Zeke could be. He'd talk about anything. A hawk screeched overhead and she saw Zeke point up to it and Reid raised his head up to look. Most hawks migrated south for the winter but some stuck around, and she loved seeing them. She watched it disappear into the trees and nudged Dixie into a trot to catch up to Reid and Zeke. She rode beside them for a few minutes in silence. Cold air formed in front of the horses' nostrils. It was a bitterly cold day.

"We can go through the trees there." She pointed to the area. "There are some great trees in that group."

Reid nodded. "All right. Is it me or is the snow getting heavier?"

"I think it is, so we need to get a move on."

"I want to build a snowman, Mama," Zeke said disappointment in his voice.

"We can't, baby. We need to get back before this gets worse. Tomorrow, we'll build one in the yard, okay?"

"But..." Zeke started to whine.

"It'll be fun to build one in the front yard, Z-man. You can look at it every day," Reid said.

"Will you come over tomorrow and help me make one?"

Reid glanced at Lucy and back to Zeke. "I don't know if I can make it."

"Why not?" She wondered if he had someone else that he'd rather spend the day with, and found she didn't like the idea.

"I don't want to wear out my welcome, Lucy."

"I don't see that happening, Reid Callahan." She tried to hide her smile and so nudged her horse into a run so he wouldn't see her pink cheeks too. Of course, she could have blamed it on the cold. She stopped Dixie right before the line of trees and dismounted. Reid stopped and handed Zeke to her then dismounted. She watched as he pulled the axe from the saddlebag and walked to her. She looked down at his feet and shook her head.

"You cowboys and your boots...you should have worn something different for being out in the snow, Reid. You should have known that the snow would be deeper up here."

"Okay, Mom. I get it."

Lucy gasped and leaned down to pick up some snow, forming it into a ball before throwing it in his direction. She missed him but he saw her, and laughed.

"I hope you weren't aiming for me." He stood there ginning at her and she couldn't stop staring at him. The man was drop dead gorgeous, and sexy as sin. She might be standing in snow, in thirty-degree weather, but she was suddenly burning up. She turned her back to him.

"Lucy?" His voice caressed over her body from behind her. She shook her head. He placed his hands on her shoulders and turned her around to face him. "What is it?"

"Nothing. Really. I'm fine." She gazed up at him. She saw his eyes glance down to her lips and she couldn't stop herself from licking them. He groaned and started to lower his head.

"Mama? I'm getting cold. Hurry."

Reid grinned at her. "For a second, I forgot we weren't alone."

Lucy laughed. "Me too. Come on! Let's find a tree for your parents."

She trudged through the deepening snow with Zeke and Reid following.

"I like this one," Reid said from behind her. She stopped and turned around. He was pointing at a gorgeous Douglas fir that had to stand close to twelve feet tall.

"It's beautiful." Lucy walked back to stand beside him.

"I like it, let's go," Zeke said, making them laugh.

"I thought you wanted to build a snowman," Reid asked him tipping his hat back a bit.

"Tomorrow. When you come over. Hurry. Mama, I have to pee."

"I thought you went before we came out here?"

"Yep, but I gotta go again." He started hopping up and down.

"Take him somewhere and I'll start cutting the tree," Reid told her with a grin.

"Come on, Zeke. Let's go over here." Lucy led her son away to a more private place behind a tree. A few minutes later, they rejoined Reid. The tree was just beginning to fall. Reid lay on the cold, wet ground and chopped at the tree.

Lucy watched as he slid out from under it, covered in snow. He put his hand against the tree and pushed until it fell over. He grinned at her.

"I'll get the rope and then we can go."

A little while later, they started back to the house with Reid's horse pulling the tree behind them. Lucy was freezing. Her teeth were starting to chatter and she envied her son staying warm against Reid's chest. The snow was accumulating and getting deeper by the minute, even as they got closer to the house. It was going to be a bad snow. She heard Reid burst out laughing at something Zeke said and it brought a smile to her lips. Finally, she saw the barns through the snow.

She rode Dixie into the barn, but Reid rode Acer over to his truck so he wouldn't have to drag the tree from the barn. Lucy had RJ put her horse up since she was so cold. Zeke was still with Reid. She walked from the barn and hurried toward them. Reid turned to lead Acer to the barn with Zeke still in the saddle. Lucy stopped beside them.

"You come with me, Zeke. It's getting way too cold." She reached up and pulled him down from atop the horse. "Let RJ put Acer up, Reid. Come inside and get warm. I'll make more coffee."

"Are you sure? I can rub Acer down."

"I know but you have to be cold." She looked down at his cowboy boots. "Especially your feet. Come on inside." Carrying Zeke, she hurried up the steps to the porch.

Once inside, she removed Zeke's coat, hat, and mittens. He sat on the floor and pulled his boots off. She removed her own boots off and hung their coats up.

"Can I have hot chocolate, Mama?"

"Of course you can. Let me make some coffee first." Lucy moved to make a pot of coffee and then she would start on Zeke's hot chocolate.

"Okie dokie. Can Reid stay overnight?"

"Uh, no. He has a home to go to."

"But it's bad out."

The boy was too wise beyond his years. "I know, baby. But Reid is a big boy and he knows how to drive in snow."

"Okay."

The door opened and Reid stepped into the kitchen. Lucy felt as if she couldn't breathe. *What is wrong with you?* She refused to look at him as he took his hat, coat, and gloves off but ended up doing just that...out of the corner of her eye, of course. He pulled a chair out, sat down, and removed his boots. She saw him glance toward the living room, and then back at her.

"Do you want me to make a fire?"

"Sure. It will help us warm up. There's wood in the cubbyhole beside the fireplace."

Reid stared at her for a few seconds, and then left the kitchen. Her breath whooshed out. Damn man. He was too hot for her peace of mind. Zeke followed him leaving her alone which was fine because she needed some solitude right now. *Would he kiss her again tonight?* She moaned thinking about it. The real question was would she let him. *You know damn well you will!*

Lucy removed the hot chocolate from the microwave then poured cups of coffee for her and Reid. After placing the cups on a tray, she took a deep breath and walked into the living room.

Chapter Four

Reid placed logs on top of the kindling and lit a match to it. The flames soon crackled and snapped around the logs. Orange and blue flames reached up toward the flue. The scent of burning wood filled the room. He reached for the poker and moved the logs around. He turned when he heard Lucy enter the room. She carried a tray. He set the poker down then walked to her, took the tray from her, and set it on the coffee table.

"Thank you," she said softly.

"You're welcome," he said just as quietly. She was so beautiful it broke his heart to know he could never have her.

Lucy smiled at him, moved to the sofa, and sat down beside Zeke. "Do you want to see if there's a Christmas movie on?"

"Yes, please." Zeke giggled then he looked at Reid. "Can you drive in snow, Reid?"

"I sure can, Z-man. Why do you ask?" Reid took a seat on the sofa.

"If you can't, you can stay with us tonight."

Reid looked at Lucy. She shrugged and blew on the steaming cup of hot chocolate before holding it out to her son. "I told him you could drive in snow."

"If I'd known that's why he was asking, I would have said no."

Lucy looked startled.

"I'm sorry, Lucy. That was out of line."

"It's all right," she said in a low voice not much

more than a whisper.

"Mama? I'm sleepy."

"Maybe you should take a nap then." Lucy stood and lifted him into her arms.

"Bye, Reid. See you tomorrow."

"Okay, Zeke. Tomorrow." Reid leaned his head back and closed his eyes. He shouldn't come back tomorrow. Zeke was beginning to get too attached to him. It was bad enough he was already far too attached to the boy.

Lucy re-entered the room and Reid stood. "I'd better get going. It's getting bad out there."

She tilted her head. "What were you laughing at on the way back? What did Zeke say?"

Reid scowled for a brief moment wondering if he should tell her, and then laughed. "He told me he made the snow yellow."

Lucy burst out laughing. "He was surprised when it happened. That was the first time he'd peed in snow."

Reid chuckled. "He's a good kid, Lucy. You've done a good job with him on your own."

"He is a good boy."

"Because of you. I really need to get going," he said but didn't move.

"I know," she whispered. Their eyes met across the room.

Reid walked toward her, stopped, and glanced up. "Maybe you should step out from under that mistletoe before I get there."

A grin tugged at her lips. "Why would I do that, Reid?"

Reid hissed in a breath and stepped in front of her. He reached his hand out and tugged on her ponytail, pulling her closer to him.

"I'm not sure this is a good idea," he murmured.

"All I've thought about is that kiss, Reid."

"Me too," he said as he lowered his head so his lips were barely touching hers. He waited.

When she stood on her toes, he grinned against her lips, and then took her mouth in a deep kiss. He groaned when she touched her tongue to his. Her arms wrapped around his neck and he placed his hands on her hips pulling her against him. His cock snapped to attention. He dragged his mouth from hers and moved it across her cheek to her jaw and down to her neck.

"God, Lucy. I want you so much," he said in the crook of her neck.

"I want you too, Reid." She pulled back from him and stared up into his eyes. "Want to take a nap with me?"

Reid raised an eyebrow. "Sure. Afterwards." He swept her up in his arms and headed in the direction she pointed. Inside the room, he stopped, staring at the bed.

"It's a new bed, Reid. This isn't the one I shared with Zeke."

Reid blew out a breath. "Thank God." Yet, he still didn't move.

"Are you going to stare at the bed or take me to it?"

Reid frowned. "Were you always such a smartass?"

Lucy laughed. "Yes. You just didn't talk to me enough to find out. Why is that?"

Reid moved to the bed, lay her down in the center of it, and gazed down at her. "Because I got tongue-tied any time you were around. I wanted you so much, and I thought if I talked to you, you'd realize it."

She lifted up on her elbows. "You wanted me? Back then?"

Reid sat on the edge of the bed. "Since the first time I saw you."

She sat up and wrapped her arms around his neck. "I didn't know."

"It wouldn't have made a difference, Lucy. You belonged to Zeke."

"Lie down with me, Reid." She kissed his lips quickly and lay back down.

"Please be sure about this, Lucy."

"I'm very sure. Aren't you?"

Reid blew out a laugh. "Never been more sure of anything in my life, darlin'."

He lay down beside her and pressed his lips to hers. Her mouth opened to allow him in. He moved his tongue into her mouth and groaned when she tangled hers with his. Her hands slid down his chest to the bottom of his T-shirt and rolled it up, and over his head. Her hands on his skin made him tremble. She ran her fingernails down his hard pecs to his six-pack stomach.

"Reid, you're beautiful," Lucy said as she leaned in and kissed his chest. Her hands moved to his belt. She placed her hand over his hard dick straining against his jeans. She lifted her eyes to his. "Absolutely beautiful."

Reid kissed her hard while moving his hand over her breast. She arched her back and moaned. It was driving him insane. He'd wanted this for so long. He slid his hand down to the bottom of her shirt and lifted it over her head. He growled low in his throat when he saw the purple bra barely containing her breasts.

"Lucy, you take my breath away," he whispered as he unhooked the front clasp. Her breasts fell free and he almost wept. "I knew you would."

He leaned down, took her nipple into his mouth, and suckled. He felt her fingers comb through his hair. She clenched her fists to hold him to her. She didn't need to. He sure as hell wasn't going anywhere. He wanted to worship this woman like no other.

"Reid, please..." she moaned.

He raised his head and looked into her beautiful face. "Please, what?"

"I need you, Reid."

"I need you too, darlin', but I'm going to go over every inch of you and savor all of you."

He lowered his head and smiled when she growled. He slid his hand to the snap of her jeans and unhooked it. He slowly lowered the zipper. He was killing himself by being patient, but he didn't want to take her fast and hard...not this time, not the first time. He moved down her legs and stood at the end of the bed. She raised her head to look at him and seeing the desire on her face almost had him coming in his jeans. He grabbed the bottom of her jeans and pulled on them. Lucy lifted her hips to help him. He tossed them across the room and stared down at her purple bikini panties. He thanked God right then for creating this incredibly beautiful woman. She crooked her finger at him making him grin. He crawled up between her legs and kissed her flat belly making her gasp. He was so hard he ached, but he had to taste her. All over.

He pulled on her panties with his teeth, hooked his fingers into the sides, and dragged them down her legs before dropping them to the floor. He stared down at her dark strip of curls revealed to him and couldn't wait to taste the treasure they hid from view. He kissed her legs making her squirm as he made his way toward his destination. He spread her legs and hooked them over his shoulders. He put his nose against her curls and inhaled then he moved his tongue through them. She gasped and clutched at his hair.

"Reid," she hissed before moaning.

He moved his tongue teasing her. He chuckled when she pulled his hair again.

"I'll get there, darlin'. Hold on," he said.

"You're killing me, Reid Callahan," she growled at him, making him smile.

"Payback's a bitch, baby. I've wanted you for years." He moved his tongue up and down between her wet slit. "You're getting so wet for me. Only for me."

"Yes Reid, only for you." She moaned then sat up grabbing his hair again. "Damn you, Reid Callahan. I swear I'll get you back for this."

Reid burst out laughing. "All right, darlin'," he said right before he used his thumbs to separate her slit and place his mouth over her clitoris.

Lucy fell back against the bed while he worked his magic. He sucked on her and rubbed his teeth against her. When he inserted his finger, he moved it against her G-spot while he teased her clitoris. Her moans were making him crazy with desire. He felt her inner muscles clench around his finger. He raised his eyes to see her pulling the pillow over her face as she screamed when her orgasm ripped through her.

Reid pulled back and stood. He slid his jeans off, retrieved a condom from his wallet, and rolled it on. He took a deep breath, crawled up her body, and inched into her. She tossed the pillow aside and stared up at him. He pressed his lips to hers and thrust the rest of the way in making her gasp. Her legs wrapped around his waist and she moved her hips in rhythm with his. He clasped her hands in his and held them by her head.

"I'm not going to last, Lucy," he growled through gritted teeth then groaned trying his best to hold back.

"Faster. Harder. Reid...please."

Reid did as she asked. It wasn't long before he felt her clench around his dick. He stared into her face and watched the flush roll over her skin. Her head tilted back and she started gasping for air. Reid knew she was there. He moved harder against her and slammed his lips down on hers as she cried out. He groaned into her mouth and came.

Reid tried to catch his breath as he put his face against her neck. She was breathing hard too. He raised his head and lightly kissed her lips. Her eyes fluttered open and she stared up at him. He gazed into her eyes feeling happier than he'd been in years. Her lips lifted into a beautiful and satisfied smile.

"That was...fantastic, Reid," she said on an exhalation.

He leaned down and kissed her again. "I

agree."

He moved off her and lay beside her. She placed her arm across his waist and laid her head on his shoulder. God, he could get so used to this. He wrapped his arms around her and held her tight.

"What do you do now, Reid? Since you retired, I mean."

"I have a small farm in Butte. I grow feed for other ranchers."

"Do you miss the rodeo?"

"Sometimes, although I still follow the circuit."

She raised her head and looked at him. "I thought you retired?"

"I am retired. I haven't ridden since I last won the championship two years ago, but I love the excitement in the arenas."

"It does seem electric, doesn't it?"

"Yes. It will always be in my blood, but I'm getting too old to ride anymore."

"I'm glad. I wouldn't want something to happen to you."

He blew out a breath, this wasn't something he wanted to talk about with her. "I'd better go, Lucy. I'm sure the snow is getting worse."

Reid sat up and swung his legs over the bed then stood to get his boxer briefs and jeans. After pulling them on, he picked up his T-shirt and boots, walked back to the bed, and stared down at her. She lay there with a smile on her face and her gorgeous naked body calling to him. He felt his cock twitching again.

"If it's too bad, you can stay the night. You'd just have to be out of my bed before Zeke wakes up," she said as she sat up against the headboard, smiling at him.

Reid stood there staring at her. He wanted her again. *Shit!* How in the hell was that even possible? After sex, he usually tore out of wherever before the woman got ideas but with Lucy, he wanted to stay. He wanted her to get ideas. He dropped his boots and shirt. She laughed low in her throat.

"Damn it, Lucy."

"I need a shower. How about you," she asked him as she got out of the bed and walked naked toward her bathroom. He couldn't keep his eyes off her perfect ass. He lowered the zipper on his jeans, shucked them and his boxer briefs, and followed her to the bathroom.

****

Lucy glanced over her shoulder to see Reid following her. She allowed her eyes to skim down that perfect body. Who'd ever have guessed what was under those clothes he wore? Reid had one hell of a body. Those hard pecs and that six-pack stomach made her mouth water. Zeke had never been built like Reid was. She mentally shook her head. Now was not the time to think of Zeke.

She reached into the shower and turned it on. Steam quickly filled the room. She smiled as Reid walked toward her. She looked down and her mouth honestly did water when she saw he was hard again. Oh, yes. Reid Callahan definitely had a great body. Every single inch of him was breathtaking.

"You keep looking at me like that and we won't even make it into the shower."

Lucy laughed. "I need a shower and I want to share it with you."

"Shit. I don't have any more condoms."

"I'm on the pill to keep my periods regular. You don't need a condom."

"I don't have sex without one," Reid muttered.

Lucy shrugged and stepped into the shower. "Suit yourself, big guy."

She could hear him muttering under his breath then the door opened, and he stepped in.

"Reid, I haven't been with anyone since Zeke died and if you always use a condom, I'd say we're safe."

"You haven't been with anyone in three years?"

"No. I never wanted anyone. Now, I just want you." She wrapped her arms around his neck as he lifted her up.

"I'm not sure I'll ever get enough of you," he whispered against her lips.

"I don't have a problem with that," she said as she pressed her lips to his. He took control and deepened the kiss. When his tongue moved into her mouth, she moaned long and low. He put his arms under her legs and spread her wide. She gasped when he thrust into her. He leaned her against the wall and pumped into her, hard.

"Shit, this is going to be over too soon. Are you with me?" His words were a growl in her ear.

"Yes. Oh God, yes Reid." She nipped at his shoulder with her teeth. When her orgasm hit her, she was glad he was holding her up because she would have fallen otherwise. She felt him throbbing inside her as he came. He put his forehead against hers and tried to catch his breath. She laughed. "Wow."

"Damn, I'm sorry," he whispered.

She smiled. "For what?"

"That was over too soon."

"It was perfect, Reid." She kissed his neck and moved her lips up to his ear where she took the lobe into her mouth and sucked on it. He moaned and moved his mouth to hers. She loved the way he kissed—especially those deep, toe-curling ones.

"I could've sworn I said I was leaving."

Lucy burst out laughing. "Well, that changed quickly. I told you that you can stay tonight if it's bad."

He pulled away from her. "We'll see how it is once we get done in here. Right now, I want to wash you." He picked up the soap and rubbed it between his palms building up a sudsy lather. He grinned at her as he turned her around and began washing her back.

Lucy closed her eyes and gave in to the feel of his hands on her but couldn't help wonder why he seemed in such a hurry to leave. Still, it was a long while before they left the bathroom.

****

Reid entered the kitchen and peered out the back door. The snow had accumulated a good bit but not to the point where he was stranded. He could leave. Thing was, he didn't want to—not yet. He wanted to stay as long as Lucy would let him. He combed his fingers through his wet hair. *Christ, the sex was better than I'd ever imagined!*

Reid had been with his share of women, maybe more than his share but not one of them made him feel the way sex with Lucy did. He wanted to stay buried inside her forever.

"Is the snow deep?" Lucy's voice startled him

from behind.

He spun around to face her and he felt as if he couldn't get enough oxygen into his lungs. He stared into her eyes, and then she tilted her head. "Reid?"

"Uh, yeah, it's getting deep...but I can still drive in it. I can get home, no problem."

"That's a shame," she murmured as she closed the distance between them, stopping in front of him.

"Damn it, Lucy. You're killing me here," he groaned and closed his eyes. He felt her need for him to stay crowd the air around him, but why did she want him to stay? Was she lonely? She missed Zeke and he was the next best thing?

"I just think that was a great way to spend a snowy afternoon. You can stay or go. I understand if you want to get home."

"I don't want to leave, but I do need to get the tree home before it gets too buried under the snow in the bed of the truck."

"Okay." She wrapped her arms around his waist and put her face against his neck. He automatically encircled his arms around her. He laid his cheek on her head. Reid wanted her to want him to stay because she wanted him as much as he wanted her.

"I'll go out and start the truck to warm it up. I'll be right back." He kissed the top of her head.

"All right." She pulled out of his arms, turned, and left the room. Reid's eyes followed her until she disappeared.

He put his hat, coat, and gloves on, and headed out the door. The cold air filled his lungs as he took a deep breath. He walked down the steps, brushed snow from the door, and window before opening the truck door then climbed inside to start the truck. Once it started, he sat there staring at the snow-covered windshield. *What the fuck are you doing, Callahan? She's Zeke's wife.*

"Zeke is dead," he said aloud but it didn't make him feel better.

For years, he'd wanted Lucy but he kept it to himself because Zeke was his friend—his best friend. He couldn't lust after his best friend's wife, yet he had. Anytime he saw her, he had desired her. There had been so many times when Zeke invited him to the ranch, but he'd declined more often than not. He couldn't be around Lucy and see her touching Zeke when all he wanted was to feel her hands on him. It had been bad enough when she'd been at the rodeo and he'd had to watch her kiss Zeke before she left to find her seat. He wanted her kisses and her touch. Now that he'd had both, how could he walk away?

He remembered his father's words about Lucy wanting something different from what she'd had with Zeke. Was he too much like Zeke? Did she only have sex with him because he reminded her of Zeke? His old friend, a memory, and a reminder of what she'd lost.

Reid glanced toward the back door. He should just go now and not come back. He shook his head in disgust. He'd already promised the Z-man he'd come back tomorrow to build a snowman with him. His fist hit the steering wheel. *Dumbass! You just couldn't keep your hands off her, could you?*

He pulled his glove-covered hands down his face. *Just go!*

He put the truck in gear and glanced toward the door again. Lucy stood there in the open doorway staring at him and he had the feeling she knew he was thinking of running. He put the truck back in Park, opened the door, and climbed out. He walked up the steps and stopped at the top. She stepped forward, her arms wrapped protectively around her because of the cold, he assumed—he hoped.

"You were going to leave, weren't you?"

"Yes. Things shouldn't have happened like that...it wasn't...I feel so guilty about this, Lucy." He jerked back when she punched him in the chest.

"Don't. I don't feel guilty. I don't feel like it shouldn't have happened. Zeke has been gone for a long time now. We're two consenting adults, Reid. It's not like we're cheating on him."

"It feels like it to me," Reid mumbled.

"Fine then, just go, Reid. I don't need this. I don't need you to make me feel like a quick lay on a cold day. I told you I haven't been with anyone since Zeke. It's not like I'm sleeping with any man who comes along. I-I've always been attracted to you and—" Her words stopped on a squeal when he grabbed her arms and pulled her against him.

"Say that again," he demanded, his ears needing to hear her say it again to believe it.

"What? That I've always been attracted to you?" He nodded. "It's the truth. I have been since the first time I met you. I always wondered what would've happened if I'd met you first."

"Damn it, Lucy. I..."

"You sure say that a lot, Reid." Lucy scowled at him.

"Mama?"

Lucy pulled away from him turning to the open doorway behind her. "I'm here, baby. I'll be right there." She turned to Reid again, wrapping her arms around herself. "It might be better if you leave as soon as your truck is warmed up. I don't want to have to explain too much to Zeke. If you don't want to come back anymore then we'll make up an excuse as to why you won't be back tomorrow." She turned on her heel and entered the kitchen, closing the door.

Reid swore under his breath. She was angry. Could he screw this up any worse? He returned to his truck feeling like a rotten heel.

Chapter Five

The next day, Reid was sure he must be out of his mind as he drove to the Rolling A. It was still snowing and getting deeper by the minute but he'd promised Zeke yesterday he'd be there, if he could drive. When Zeke had said he knew he could, there was no way Reid wouldn't get there. Besides, he needed to see Lucy. He only hoped she wasn't still mad at him. *Shit!*

He drove up the driveway and pulled the truck to a stop by the back porch. The snow was now coming down harder now. *Wonderful!* He shut the engine off and sat there staring at the door. He had just about convinced himself to leave when the back door opened, and he saw Lucy and Zeke standing in the doorway, watching him. Taking a deep breath, he threw the cab door open and climbed out. He walked up the steps, knocked the snow off his boots, and entered the kitchen behind them. He spun around to face Lucy who was leaning up against the counter when she chuckled. He raised his eyebrow at her. She shrugged her shoulders.

"You were out there fighting with yourself, weren't you Reid," she asked letting her gaze fall to the floor instead of holding his.

"How would you even know that?"

She shrugged again. "I saw you pull up and by the way you were wrapping your hands around the steering wheel, I knew you were in a battle with yourself."

"Yeah, well, I'm here now." He looked to Zeke

and put on a false smile. "Are you ready to build a snowman, Z-man?"

"Yep," Zeke yelled, hopping up and down on one foot.

Reid chuckled. "Get your coat, hat, and mittens, and let's do this."

"Hurry up, Zeke. It's getting bad out and Reid will need to leave soon."

When Zeke ran off, Reid turned to her. "I just got here, Lucy. Are you trying to get rid of me already?"

"Nope." She moved closer to him and stood on her toes to put her lips close to his. "I'm actually hoping you'll get stranded here, and have to spend the night."

Reid groaned, and started to put his hands on her waist when Zeke suddenly ran back into the kitchen. He skidded to a halt with eyes wide in his cherub face.

"Mama? Were you kissing Reid?"

"Shit," Reid muttered.

Lucy laughed. "Don't I kiss you to warm you up? Reid was cold."

"I'm sure as hell not anymore," Reid whispered.

"Yep. Did you get warm, Reid?"

"Hot is more like it, Z-man. Your mom is good at that." Lucy punched his arm, making him laugh.

"Come here, baby, and I'll help you get ready."

Reid leaned close to her ear. "You can whisper that in my ear anytime. Were you serious about what you said yesterday?"

Lucy glanced up from where she was helping Zeke zip up his jacket. "You got it, cowboy."

Reid wasn't sure how he was feeling about things now. He nearly groaned at the thought of her warming him up but liked that she wasn't angry with him about leaving yesterday, and that she admitted being attracted to him all these years. He needed to talk to her—alone. Of course, that was easier said than done with Zeke around. "You're more evil than I'd ever realized."

She tossed her hair over her shoulder and stared up at him. "You have no idea." She handed Zeke a carrot. "Here, Zeke...for the snowman's nose."

"Okay, I'm ready. Let's go," Zeke said and ran for the door.

"Good luck keeping up with him," Lucy said with a sly grin.

"You're not coming out with us?"

"No way. This was your idea. I'll watch from the window in the living room."

Reid nodded. "Yep. Evil." He kissed her quickly. "You and me, we need to talk."

Then he headed out the door after Zeke.

****

Lucy smiled as she walked to the living room with her cup of coffee and sat in the rocking chair next to the window. She watched as Zeke ran around in the snow and she saw Reid shaking his head in what had to be wonder, as he watched him. He stooped down, picked up some snow, made a ball, and tossed it at Zeke hitting him in the chest. Zeke stopped and stared at him then picked up some snow and ran full-speed at Reid hitting him in the legs with it. She could hear Zeke's laughter through the window. He squealed when Reid caught him and tossed him into the air. She shook her head. It didn't look as if they were as interested in building a snowman as they were in having a snowball fight. Boys...and it didn't matter their age.

Finally, they started working on a snowman and had one put together in no time. She watched as Reid dug through the snow in the driveway. He found gravel for the eyes and mouth. He was good with Zeke and that had her worried. She didn't want her son becoming too attached to a man who already had a life somewhere else. She couldn't even be sure that Reid didn't have someone else waiting at home for him. He hadn't said he hadn't had sex recently, only that he always used a condom. He hadn't responded when she told him she had always been attracted to him. Was she just a holiday fling? Another trophy for Reid to win that Zeke had once won.

She stood and walked to her bedroom returning with a scarf. She opened the front door and stepped onto the porch.

"Zeke, come get this scarf for your snowman's neck," she called to him.

"Okay, Mama." He ran toward the steps and fell face first into the snow. Lucy started to run down the steps.

"I got him," Reid told her as he strode to Zeke. He picked him up and laughed at Zeke's snow-covered face. Lucy burst out laughing when Zeke pushed a handful of snow in Reid's face. Reid looked up at her and his eyes narrowed. "I'd go back inside if I were you," he said in a menacing voice.

She widened her eyes as she observed him

pick up snow and form a ball. She ran for the door and slammed it behind her just as she heard the snowball hit the door. She leaned back against the door to catch her breath. *And he calls her evil!*

She laughed as she returned to the living room to watch from the window. She jumped back when a snowball hit the window. That man was in so much trouble. Grinning, Lucy returned to the rocking chair where she watched her son and the man, who was wiggling his way into her heart and her son's life, play in the snow.

She was already half in love with him now and it would be so easy to fall the rest of the way. But what did she really know about him? He said he was retired from the rodeo, but he was still young enough to return to the circuit if the urge grabbed him. He said he wouldn't, but could she believe that? The thought of him losing his life, the way Zeke had, was something she couldn't grasp. Of course, that was the least of her worries since when the holidays were over, he would leave and there was no guarantee he would ever return.

She was in so much trouble here. She knew she couldn't love another bull rider, but then he might actually be done with that world. What about the life he has now? Would that keep him away just as easily as the rodeo circuit? It might not be as dangerous but it wouldn't include her.

Damn you, Zeke for leaving me! If he were still here, she wouldn't be having these thoughts about Reid. She'd done just fine without seeing him for three years. Of course, in the beginning, she'd had her anger to aid her. The infatuation had disappeared but now he was here, back in her life and she had no idea if that was a good thing or bad.

Her heart nearly stopped when she heard Zeke scream. She looked out the window but he wasn't hurt, he was only having fun. Reid was chasing him. Zeke's little legs trudged through the deepening snow while Reid acted as if he couldn't catch him. Anytime he got close, Zeke would scream. She could see from here how red his cheeks and nose were getting. She grinned happily when Reid caught him, and tossed him over his shoulder. Tears formed in her eyes and she glanced upwards as if to heaven.

"Are you watching, Zeke? Your son is having a ball with your best friend. Somehow, I think you'd approve." She looked back outside and saw them heading toward the back of the house.

Lucy heard the back door open and so headed out to the kitchen. She stopped in her tracks when she looked at the two males standing in her kitchen, covered in snow. She raised an eyebrow at Reid.

"I guess we should go out on the porch and knock this snow off us, Z-man. Mom is giving us the evil eye," Reid said with a smirk.

Zeke put his hands over his mouth and giggled. "Mama, are you giving us the..." He glanced up at Reid. "What was it?"

Reid grinned down at him. "The evil eye."

"Yeah, that's it. Are you, Mama?"

"I am. Out!" She pointed to the porch.

Reid and Zeke laughed but wandered back out to the porch. Lucy stood in the doorway and watched them. She laughed when Reid brushed the snow off Zeke while he spun around, giggling. When Reid stomped his boots to knock the excess snow off, Zeke copied him marching in place doing little actually to rid his boots of snow. Reid knocked the snow from his hat and coat and Zeke watched him, clapping his mittens together when Reid smacked his gloved hands against each other. Together, they reentered the kitchen. Reid pulled out a chair and sat down to remove his boots. Meanwhile, she busied herself relieving Zeke of his wet coat, hat, and mittens before sitting him in a chair to remove his boots.

"I'm surprised to see you in any boots other than your cowboy boots," she said glancing over at Reid.

"I had a feeling I was going to be in the snow quite a while," he said as he unlaced his hiker boots.

"Smart move. Zeke, do you want hot chocolate? Reid? Coffee?"

"Coffee sounds good," Reid told her.

"I want coffee like Reid," Zeke said, now running around the kitchen table.

Lucy looked at Reid. He stopped unlacing his boots and stared at Zeke then looked at Lucy.

"I'll have hot chocolate."

Lucy smiled. "Sounds good. You two go warm up by the fire and I'll bring it in."

"Let's go, Z-man. We're being banished from the kitchen."

"What's banished mean," Zeke asked him as they left the kitchen.

Lucy took a deep breath and went about making each of them a cup of hot chocolate. She glanced out the window located above the sink and smiled when she saw the snow coming down more heavily. She wanted Reid to spend the night and she was going to do her best to talk him into it.

****

Reid added logs to the fire and moved them around with the poker. He glanced over his shoulder to see Zeke bouncing up and down on the couch. He grinned and shook his head. His dad had been right. Zeke was a tornado, just as his father had been. The smile left his face when he thought of Zeke. His friend was missing the most amazing experience ever, even better than riding the meanest bull. He knew he would've loved his son so much, just as Reid was beginning to love him. The idea of this little boy having never known his father tore at his heartstrings. Just like his mama did. Lucy was the woman he wanted in his life. She was the reason he'd never settled down. No other woman ever compared to her. None ever would.

He stared into the fire, wondering where this was going. He was only here through New Year's Day. He had a farm to run and he had to get back to it. He watched the flames roll over the wood but didn't really see it.

So why are you thinking of not going home right away?

"I'm not," he muttered.

"Not what?" Lucy said from behind him.

Reid spun around feeling as if she'd caught him doing something wrong. "Nothing...just thinking out loud, I guess."

He took a cup of hot chocolate from the tray she held out to him. He watched her set it on the coffee table, and handed Zeke his cup.

"Be careful, it's still hot," she warned Zeke.

"Okay, Mama. I'll blow on it." He grinned up at her, and then looked over to Reid. "You better blow on it, Reid. Mama makes it hot."

"Mama sure does," Reid said as he shifted his eyes toward her. He smiled when she blushed.

"Stop," she said.

Reid chuckled. He took a sip of his too hot cocoa, and watched Lucy fuss over Zeke and his cup. He liked watching her be a mother.

As the day wore on, they relaxed in the living room watching Christmas movies until Zeke started to drift off. Lucy stood and picked him up.

"Let's get you to bed, Z-man." She glanced at Reid. "I'll be right back."

"I'll be here."

She stared at him for a few seconds then nodded, and walked off with Zeke. Reid stared at the fire. He'd come to a decision. He seriously needed to stop coming here. This, whatever this was, couldn't go anywhere and he was just falling more in love with both of them. He sighed. He should have just stayed away, never accepted the invitation to dinner, and sure as hell never should have kissed her. If he hadn't kissed her, they wouldn't have ended up in bed together.

He ran his hand over his whiskered jaw and swore under his breath. This was wrong on so many levels. Yes, he felt guilty, but also scared that he was just a Zeke substitute. Now he wondered how he was he going to leave them behind after having experienced two of the best days of his life with them. Christmas was in two days, and he had family obligations but all he wanted to do was be with Lucy and Zeke. He'd love to see the look on Zeke's face Christmas morning when he saw the pony Santa was bringing him. Reid smiled with sadness thinking how it wasn't his moment to enjoy. He turned when he heard Lucy behind him.

"Are you all right?" she asked him.

"Yeah, I was just thinking about how excited Zeke's going to be when he sees his pony Christmas morning."

"Can you come over Christmas day?"

"I wish I could, but I have to be at my parents' for the day."

"What about later?"

"I suppose I could."

Lucy spun away from him. "Don't do me any favors, Reid Callahan."

Reid grasped her elbow and turned her to face him. "Hey, I'd love to be here, but don't you have family obligations too?"

"I'll be going to my parents' for breakfast and my in-laws' in the afternoon, but we'll be here alone after that."

"All right then, I'll come over, but I want to get Zeke something. What can I get him?"

"You don't have to do that..."

"I know that, Lucy. I want to."

She smiled up at him and his heart seemed to stop. "He said he wants a coat like the one you wear."

"My sheepskin? What size?"

"Reid, they're too expensive."

"What size?" He stared her down. He wasn't going to be dissuaded.

80

Giving in, Lucy told him where to get the coat and what size then she walked to him and put her arms around his neck, stood on her toes and kissed him.

"How about a nap, cowboy?" she whispered against his lips.

"Sure. Later, first...did you really mean what you said about having always been attracted to me?" he asked her, not sure he really wanted to hear the answer.

"Yes, I really meant it. I loved Zeke, I won't deny that, but had you come into my life first...well, things might have gone a different way." She smiled up at him and suddenly, he didn't feel so guilty. He kissed her, picked her up, and carried her to the bedroom. He pushed the door shut behind him and walked to the bed. Her fingers in his hair were driving him insane. He placed his knee on the bed and lowered her to the center. He pulled his T-shirt off and lay down beside her. Her fingernails skimmed down his chest to his stomach.

"Where do you get all these muscles, Reid?" She leaned forward and kissed his chest making him draw in a breath.

"I work hard on the farm and exercise." He wrapped his hand around her wrist. "You're killing me, darlin'."

"They're very sexy." She kissed down his stomach. When he reached for her shirt, she stopped him. "Remember when I said I'd pay you back for teasing me?"

Reid ran his hands through her hair. "I don't recall that."

Lucy laughed softly. "Liar."

Reid held his breath when she unsnapped his jeans and lowered the zipper. He was already hard. He jerked when her hand snaked inside his jeans and wrapped around his hard cock. When she removed her hand and sat up, he stared at her frowning in disappointment.

"Let's take these off," she said as she walked to the end of the bed where she pulled his jeans off, leaving him only in his boxer briefs. She then crawled up between his legs, her gaze capturing his so that he couldn't look away. "I love boxer briefs. I think they are so sexy."

"Then I'll wear them all the time," he said giving her a big smile.

"I like you better without them." She kissed his stomach making him flinch then she grabbed the waistband on his briefs and pulled them down, kissing the skin along his legs as she uncovered it.

"Lucy, I-I don't think..." He moaned. He watched her drop his boxer briefs onto the floor then drag her tongue up one thigh before switching to the other. When her hot wet tongue slid across his balls, he damn near came right that moment. His fingers tangled in her hair. "Lucy..."

"Shush...relax."

Reid blew out a laugh that sounded more like a grunt. "Easy for you to say."

Lucy raised her head and looked at him. "Payback, cowboy." Then she grinned and without taking her eyes from his, she ran her tongue along his hard length and wrapped her hand around him. "You are so remarkable, Reid. How can something so hard, feel so soft?"

She kissed the head of his dick, and Reid couldn't stop the groan from tearing from his chest. He'd had blowjobs before but just knowing this was Lucy, had his self-control stretching to the limit, especially when she put her mouth down over him and sucked. His hips bucked.

"Lucy, baby, please."

She lifted her head only enough to give him a mischievous smile on her face. "Please, what?"

"Christ, you're evil," he muttered as he dropped his head back onto the pillow. He felt her chuckle against his hard length as she slid him into her mouth again. A moment later, when she moaned, it shot right through him.

****

Lucy had never enjoyed doing this before. Possibly because Zeke had never returned the favor yet always wanted it done on him. She had stopped doing it soon after they were married because it had all been about him. She mentally shook her head. Now was not the time to be thinking of Zeke. This time she was enjoying it so much it was making her crazy with desire. This time it was all about Reid. A man she was quickly falling deeper in love with and wanted to please him as he pleased her.

She pumped her hand up and down his length while she sucked on him. When she cupped his balls in her hand, she heard him growl and peeked up at him. He was watching her. God! He was so sexy.

"Lucy, you have to stop now," he groaned while tugging at her hair.

"No." She said the word without removing him from her mouth. She enjoyed the control, the power of what she was doing to him.

"I want to be inside you, baby. I want to come inside you."

Such simple things he said, but the words turned her on. When he would tell her in a whisper near her ear how he felt about being inside her, her whole body quivered. This time, he didn't say another word but grabbed her, tossing her down onto her belly, and making her squeal. He quickly separated her from her jeans and panties, and moved up between her legs, spreading them. He ran his finger through her wet slit. Then he lifted her hips up, and he thrust into her hard from behind. She let out a loud gasp.

"Did I hurt you," he asked her, his body stilling behind her while his voice near her ear was full of concern.

"No. No...please, Reid. Take me hard," she murmured then groaned when he slammed into her hard. He took her hands in his and placed them on the headboard. His hands wrapped tight over hers as he thrust in and out of her. He nipped gently at her shoulder and she couldn't stop shaking. She felt his lips by her ear.

"I can feel you're close. You're already squeezing around my cock. Let's do this together, baby," he groaned in ear.

Lucy thrust her hips back against him and bit her lip to keep from crying out, as her orgasm shook her to her core. Reid groaned behind her and she felt him throbbing inside her as he came. He sat back on his heels and pulled her back against him. Sweat dripped down her temples. She slid her hands up behind her until they rested around his neck. He kissed her shoulder, even as he breathed heavily against her skin.

"Are you okay?" He rested his head against hers.

"Yes. Amazing...that was amazing." She panted and leaned forward to lie down. Reid dropped down beside her on his back. She swatted at him playfully. "You just couldn't let me finish, could you?"

Reid burst out laughing. "I told you..."

"Yeah, yeah, I know...you wanted to be inside me, but you already were."

"Not what I meant and you know it. I know a lot of women don't like to do that."

Lucy sat up and stared at him. "Oh, you do, do you?"

"Shit. I'll just shut up now."

Lucy laughed, pulled a quilt up over them, and curled against him. "Let's take that nap now."

"I think I need one."

"Men. What is it with you? Zeke..." She stopped when Reid's gaze shifted to her and he stared at her. "I'm sorry. I didn't mean to..."

"It's fine. Lucy, he's a part of us."

"Yes, but now was not the time or place to mention him."

When Reid didn't say anything more, she turned on her side away from him. *Stupid! Stupid! Stupid! What were you thinking?* She hadn't been. She was just going to comment that Zeke had always fallen asleep after sex. She wasn't comparing the two men. There was no comparison. Although, she had loved Zeke, it had been the love of a young girl. What she felt for Reid was the love a woman feels for a man. Granted, Zeke had been a young man too, but perhaps she'd been too young when she met him. She never doubted her love for him, but it was never anything like what she felt for Reid now.

He was going to be leaving. After the holidays, he was going home to Butte and he hadn't mentioned anything about them getting together again. *God that hurt.* She needed him in her life. Zeke needed him too. She knew Zeke loved him. Zeke talked about Reid all the time. It seemed almost non-stop at times. His little heart was going to be broken when Reid left them—just like hers.

She unintentionally stiffened when Reid wrapped his arm around her waist and kissed the back of her shoulder. "It's fine, Lucy."

She sniffled when tears started to form. "I wasn't comparing you to him, honestly. I was just going to say he always fell asleep after..."

"Sex. You can say it. I know you had sex with him, at least once anyway. You had a baby together."

Lucy rolled to her back and stared at him. She could see he was doing his best not to laugh.

"You're real funny, Callahan."

Reid laughed. "I am, aren't I?"

"Seriously though, I wasn't comparing you."

"I know, Lucy. Zeke and I were friends, but complete opposites. Let's take a nap." He kissed her cheek and pulled her close.

Lucy nodded and laid her cheek on his chest. He was right. The two men were complete opposites and not just in looks but personalities, and the bedroom. As much as she hated to admit it, it was Zeke, who couldn't compare to Reid.

Chapter Six

Christmas morning dawned bitterly cold. Lucy loaded Zeke into his car seat even though he wasn't happy about going anywhere.

"I want to stay with my pony," he cried scowling at her as she buckled him in.

"Ezekiel Albright, you will stop right this minute. Santa will not be happy with you." Lucy had tried everything this morning to get him ready to go to her parents' home. He was having none of it.

"I don't care. I want to stay with my pony," he screamed and kicked his feet against the seat.

"All right, mister. If you don't behave so we can go see what Santa left you at Nana and Pap's, I will call Reid and tell him not to come over later." She had to bite her lip to stop the smile when she saw Zeke's eyes nearly bug out of his head.

"No, Mama. I'll be good. I want to see Reid and show him my pony."

"Good. Then let's go see Nana and Pap then we'll go see Grandma and Grandpa."

"Then we come home?"

"Yes, baby. Then we come home and Reid will come over." She grinned when Zeke clapped his hands.

After carefully maneuvering snow-covered roads, she finally arrived at her parents' home. Unbuckling Zeke was a lot easier than buckling in had been. Together, they walked hand in hand into the warm kitchen where her mother greeted them both with hugs. She helped Zeke out of his coat and hat while Lucy took her coat off and hung it on the back of a chair.

"What did Santa bring my big boy," JoAnn Woodard asked her grandson with an eager smile.

Zeke jumped up and down. "I got a pony!"

"A pony? Wow, you must have been a good boy."

Lucy snorted and laughed when her mother grinned. "He must have been, although I don't remember when."

JoAnn laughed. "I can barely remember those times with you either."

"Oh, please. I was an angel."

"An angel with horns," Edward Woodard remarked as he entered the kitchen. He hugged Lucy and then picked Zeke up. "Let's see if Santa left anything here for you."

"Okay, but we can't stay long. We have to go to my other grandma and grandpa's house then we go home and Reid will come over."

The sudden silence in the kitchen was deafening. Lucy felt the heat pour into her cheeks as her mother and father stared at her. Edward cleared his throat and left the room with Zeke. Lucy turned to her mother. JoAnn had her head tilted and a smile played around her lips.

"Would that be Reid Callahan?"

Lucy nodded. "Yes. We...I...he's...well, he's been around."

"Sounds like it."

"Oh Mom, I think I'm in love with him," Lucy said, wringing her hands together.

"It's about time you found someone new."

"But, it's Reid...the same man I tore to shreds at the cemetery."

"He's forgiven you for that, obviously. I always did like Reid."

"Yes, he's forgiven me but...what will people think?"

"That the two people who loved Zeke the most found love together." JoAnn started working on scrambling eggs, and frying bacon. "Does he feel the same way?"

"I have no idea. He hasn't said anything and he's leaving right after New Year's."

"Ask him to stay longer."

"I thought about it, but what if he doesn't feel the same and I'm just a fling for the holidays?"

"I suppose it's a possibility, but then maybe he feels the same way...won't know, unless you talk to him."

"I guess I'm just afraid of knowing the truth if it's not what I want to hear," Lucy admitted as she poured juice into glasses. "He has his life in Butte. Maybe he doesn't want a ready-made family. I'm still not sure Zeke..."

"First off, Reid Callahan is not Zeke. They may have been best friends, but I always saw a lot more maturity in Reid. Don't get me wrong, honey. I loved Zeke but he never seemed to grow up. He took too many risks when he shouldn't have. He had a wife he needed to take care of, and had he known about Zeke coming, I'm not sure he would've changed. How many nights was he out drinking with his friends while you sat home alone? Have you ever told Reid about that?"

Lucy shook her head.

"Communication is the key to any good relationship," her mother told her.

Lucy didn't know if she could tell Reid how irresponsible Zeke had been during the years they were married, but her mom was right. Zeke was always taking chances, it was no wonder he decided to take one more ride. He went out in a blaze of glory probably just as he wanted.

She drew in a deep breath and finished helping her mom prepare breakfast. It wasn't long before they were heading to Zeke's parents' house. When she entered the house, everyone smiled at her, and hugged her while someone grabbed Zeke, leading him to the living room for more gifts. Lucy found herself alone in the kitchen with Zeke's sister, Cindy.

"What's new with you, Lucy?"

"Nothing, I guess." Lucy glanced out the kitchen window.

"Oh, that sounded more like an *I've got something new going on* nothing, if you ask me." Cindy smiled at her. They'd always gotten along.

"I'm fine."

"Ha! Sounds like you have something on your mind." Cindy's eyes narrowed as she looked at her. "Or, maybe it's *someone?*"

Lucy forced a laugh. "Don't be ridiculous, Cindy."

Cindy grabbed her arm and whirled her around. "You do! Are you seeing someone?"

"What if I am?"

"I'd say it's about damn time. Zeke's been gone over three years now. You need to fall in love again, Lucy."

"You think so?"

"Of course, you're a young, beautiful woman. You need a man in your life." Cindy glanced at the doorway. "Doesn't she, Mom?"

Lucy spun around to see her mother in-law standing in the doorway. Estelle Albright smiled at her. "Yes, she does."

Estelle walked to her and hugged her. "Do you have something to tell us?"

Lucy groaned. "Zeke said something, didn't he?"

Estelle laughed and nodded. "Maybe."

Cindy stared at her mother. "What? I missed it."

"Zeke said he couldn't wait to show *Reid* his pony."

"Reid?" Cindy frowned at her mother then at Lucy.

Lucy and Estelle laughed as they watched the invisible lightbulb go on over her head when Cindy figured it out. "Reid? As in Reid Callahan?"

Lucy nodded. "Yes. Is that all right?" She didn't know why she felt she needed Zeke's family to give her permission, but she did.

"Is that all right? Are you freakin' kidding me? That man is so hot. I've always thought so. Who better for you than Reid? I think Zeke would be very happy." Cindy hugged her.

Lucy wanted to cry. She never expected that Zeke's family would be happy for her to be seeing Reid. Although, she might be jumping ahead of herself but he'd come to mean so much to her after just a few days. Was it possible to fall in love so quickly? Maybe there had always been more than just a crush for her concerning Reid.

Later, by the time she arrived home, Zeke was

asleep in his car seat. She carried him into the house and to his room. She laid him on his bed, removed his boots, hat, coat, and mittens. He didn't stir a bit. She couldn't help but wish Reid were here so they could take one of their special naps together.

After unloading all the gifts that both sets of grandparents had bestowed on Zeke and the gifts they'd bought her too, she settled in a chair to relax. She wished Reid would stick around for a while after the holidays but she knew he was going to leave eventually anyway, and her heart broke at the thought. Her mom was right about talking to him. She glanced at the clock. He would be here in two hours and she couldn't help but be nervous. She'd bought him a gift and hoped he liked it—a new Stetson. It was dark brown with a silver band around it. She thought it looked like something he would wear when she saw it.

The large turkey dinner she'd had at her in-laws was having its affects. Lucy was suddenly very sleepy. She decided to lie on the couch for a few minutes and rest. *Besides, it might make the time until Reid arrives pass faster.*

****

When Reid parked his truck at the back door, he noticed the house was dark. Lucy's SUV sat across from the back porch so he knew she had to be home. Taking a deep breath, he started to open the door to his truck when he heard a pinging sound on the roof. *Great.* Ice. He blew his breath out. His truck didn't do well in ice.

He pushed the door open, grabbing the presents on the seat beside him and made his way to the porch. He bounded up the steps and knocked on the door. When no one answered, he tried the knob to see if it was unlocked—the door opened.

"Lucy? Zeke?" No answer, so he stepped into the kitchen closing the door behind him.

He set the packages on the table and headed into the living room. He came to a halt when he saw Lucy asleep on the sofa. She looked so beautiful. Her lush lips slightly parted, and her dark hair splayed across the pillow under her head. His dick twitched at the thought of seeing it spread out on the pillows in her bed. He knew he'd fallen very much in love with her and now he worried how she was going to react when he told her he was leaving to prepare for a rodeo. She was going to hate him. Perhaps it was best he didn't tell her why he was leaving as originally planned even after he'd decided to stay another week.

He walked to the couch and crouched down beside it. He gently touched her face and watched her eyes flutter open. A smile lifted her lips. "Hi," she whispered.

"Hi yourself, what happened? Did the turkey do you in?"

Lucy pushed herself up into a sitting position and brushed her hair out of her face. "Yeah, something like that, long day too. How about you?"

"I'm tired, but not too tired to see you," he said as he leaned forward and took her lips in a deep kiss.

"Reid!" Zeke's voice filled the room. Reid turned just in time to catch him when the little boy threw himself at him.

"Hey, buddy. Was Santa good to you?"

"I got a pony! You have to come see my pony. He's in the barn."

"Santa didn't put him under the tree?"

Zeke giggled. "No, silly, he couldn't get him down the chimley."

"Silly me. What was I thinking? Go get your coat, hat, and mittens and we'll go see this pony of yours."

Zeke ran off down the hallway. Lucy stood and kissed Reid. He wrapped his arms around her and pulled her tightly against him. He lifted his lips from hers and gazed into her eyes.

"Am I ever going to get enough of you?"

"I hope not. Reid..."

"Okay, I'm ready," Zeke yelled as he ran into the living room.

Reid looked down at the boy's feet and grinned. "Your boots are on the wrong feet, buddy."

Zeke sat down on the floor and pulled his boots off. When he put them back on, he stood, and then hopped up and down.

"Come on, Reid." He tugged at Reid's hand.

"We'll be right back," Reid told Lucy with a big smile.

"I'll be here."

"You can come, Mama."

"I'm fine, baby. I'll get you some hot chocolate ready."

Reid winked at her and let Zeke lead him through the kitchen. Zeke stopped when he saw the presents sitting on the table.

"You can look at those when we come back,"

Reid told him. Zeke nodded, and they set off to make their way to the barn. Once there, Zeke led him to the pony in the stall. A Shetland pony stood there staring at them with big brown eyes.

"He's pretty, huh Reid?"

"That's a fine pony, Z-man." Reid told him.

"Mama is going to let me ride him when it gets warmer outside. I can't wait."

"I bet. I remember riding my first horse. I was about your age."

"Did my daddy ride when he was my age?"

Reid's heart ached at the mention of Zeke. He should be here with his wife and son on Christmas, not his best friend. "Yes, he did. We grew up together and learned to ride horses and bulls together."

"You *are* a real cowboy."

Reid laughed. "I told you, I have the hat to prove it. Let's go in and see what I brought you."

"Okay. Can you carry me?"

Reid took a deep breath and picked him up. He carried him inside the house. Lucy had coffee and hot chocolate ready.

"I think he wants to see what I brought him."

She nodded while pulling Zeke's outerwear off. "Let's see what Reid brought you, baby." She took her son by the hand, started for the living room, and then said to Reid over her shoulder. "Bring those into the living room, please."

Reid took his hat, coat, and gloves off and hung them in the laundry room then picked up the gifts, and followed her. He set the gifts down on the floor near the tree. He handed Zeke his, and then Lucy hers. She looked surprised but smiled at him.

Before opening her gift, she stood and walked to the tree, pulled a wrapped box from under it, and handed it to him.

"You didn't have to get me anything." He accepted the present with a hesitant smile.

"And you didn't have to get us anything," Lucy said with a sly smile.

Reid grinned. "Touché."

They watched Zeke rip the paper off before lifting the lid on the box. He squealed with delight when he saw the sheepskin coat just like the one Reid had. He put it on and grinned at Reid.

"You have another one there, Z-man," Reid said pointing at a second gift.

Zeke sat down and quickly tore open the other one. Inside was a black cowboy hat like his daddy's hat. Zeke put it on and Reid almost lost it. He cleared his throat in order to speak.

"You look just like your daddy. I thought you could wear that one until your...head grew enough to wear his." Reid looked over to Lucy and she had a tear rolling down her face.

She smiled at him. "They both look great on him. What do you say, Zeke?"

"Thank you, Reid."

"You're welcome, Z-man." Reid glanced at Lucy. "Open yours."

She nodded and tore open the package lifting the lid. She gasped. Inside was another sheepskin coat. She pulled it out and held it up. "Reid, this is too much," she said.

"No, it's not. You need a new coat. I've seen yours. That one will keep you warmer."

"Thank you. Open yours now."

Reid lifted the package onto his lap and tore the paper off. He lifted the lid and stared down at the Stetson inside the box. It was perfect. He raised his eyes to meet hers. "Thank you. I needed a new one."

"If you don't like it..."

"I love it, Lucy."

She blushed when he continued to stare at her. "I'm glad," she whispered.

"Mama? Can we watch *Toy Story*?"

"Of course, we can. I'll make some popcorn. You go get the movie." With an excited squeak, Zeke ran from the room. Lucy turned to Reid. "Will you stay tonight?"

Reid had hoped she would ask. He walked to her and cupped her face in his hands. "Yes."

He pressed his lips to hers, and then deepened the kiss when she opened to him. He knew if he lived to be a hundred years old, he would never get enough of this woman. He just wished he knew how to make this work—to hold on to her.

Zeke ran into the room and jumped on the couch. Together, the three of them watched the movie and after Zeke fell asleep, Reid carried him to bed and tucked him in then joined Lucy in her bed.

Chapter Seven

On New Year's Eve, Reid picked Lucy up to head into town for a party where he was sure most of the town would show up. He knocked on the back door and heard her call out for him to come in. He entered the kitchen and came to a halt when he saw her standing in the archway to the living room. His breath lodged in his throat. She looked stunning in a black dress and knee high black suede boots. His dick noticed too, making him take a deep breath to calm his desire. The dress hugged her like a second skin. It had a plunging neckline that showed her cleavage to full delicious advantage. A row of buttons ran down the front and he wanted desperately to slowly unbutton each one as he kissed every bit of skin they revealed.

"Do you like my dress," she asked him, with a sly smile on her face while turning once.

"Like it? I'd like to peel it off you." He walked to her and stopped a few feet from her because he wasn't sure if he touched her, he'd be able to stop. "You look amazing."

"You look pretty good yourself, cowboy."

Reid smirked. He was wearing a black dress shirt, jeans, and black cowboy boots. Nothing fancy...he wasn't a fancy kind of man.

"I have a feeling I'll be punching a lot of men tonight because I don't want any of them looking at you."

She put her arms around his neck and kissed his lips. She tugged on his bottom lip with her teeth. "Just remember, I'm coming home with you." She kissed his jaw and whispered in his ear. "I'll even leave the boots on when we go to bed."

Reid groaned. "Let's just skip this thing and go to bed now."

Lucy laughed. "Nope. I haven't been out in forever and Zeke is staying with his Aunt Cindy for two nights."

"Fuck. You shouldn't have told me that." He took a deep breath. Two nights, only it was his last two nights in town. "Are you ready to do this, darlin'?"

Lucy frowned up at him. "Yes. I'm a little nervous."

"Why? People know we've known each other for years. They're just going to get a hell of a surprise when I kiss you at New Year's."

Lucy laughed. "You mean to tell me that I have to wait until midnight to get a kiss?"

Reid pressed his lips to hers. "If you want, I'll kiss you all night, baby." He took her hand in his. "Come on. Let's get your coat and head out. I left the truck running to keep it warm."

"All right." She handed him her coat and he helped her into it. When he lifted her hair from under it, he kissed the back of her neck and she trembled beneath his lips. He chuckled.

"I want to kiss you from head to toe and everywhere in between, but we'll wait until we come back."

"Teaser...how am I supposed to get through the night now, Reid?"

"If I have to suffer, so do you. Let's go."

****

100

The butterflies in Lucy's stomach were fluttering in a great flight as if they had somewhere important to go. She didn't know why she was so nervous. It wasn't like she and Reid were doing anything wrong, they were both adults, and single but walking into the party was going to be hard. She hated being the center of attention and she worried they would be. It had been over three years but she hadn't been out with anyone since Zeke's death, and here she was...with Zeke's best friend.

"Relax," Reid said close to her ear.

"I'm trying. I just hate the thought of people talking about me...about us."

"Darlin', you don't have to worry about anyone. What's it matter? It's no one's business. For all they know, we're just coming here together because we're friends. You think they're going to know we've been sleeping together or something. I don't see a sign anywhere." He looked closely at her forehead before pressing a kiss to it, making her chuckle.

"No. I'm just..." She shook her head and grinned. "Oh, I don't know. Let's go."

Reid climbed out and walked around to help her out. He took her hand in his, and held onto her as they carefully walked into the town hall. Music emerged from inside, where the lights were low with an old disco ball spinning from the ceiling throwing different colored lights around the room. No one seemed to take notice of them at all.

Reid helped her with her coat and then took his off too. He walked to the girl behind the counter, and handed them to her. The girl smiled up at him and gave him tickets for the coats. Lucy watched her flirt with him, and she wanted to scream at her to back off. She turned her gaze away from them glancing around the room. Everyone seemed to be having a great time. People crowded the dance floor, while others watched and chatted.

Lucy jerked when Reid put his hand on her lower back. He led her toward a table. She inwardly cringed when she saw his parents wave to them from the table. She glanced up at Reid. "Are we going to sit with your parents?"

"Is that all right? I think your parents are sitting there too, along with Zeke's."

Lucy groaned when she saw her in-laws sitting there along with her own. Of course, they would since they all knew about her and Reid, and since they were all friends, it made sense. She just hadn't considered the possibility. She stiffened as Reid pushed her toward the smiling group at the table. She felt him lean close to her ear.

"They won't bite. I might, but they won't."

"You behave, Reid Callahan," she muttered.

Reid chuckled. "I will...for now."

Two hours later, she was laughing and having more fun than she ever thought she would. Many people had come over to her throughout the evening to hug her and tell her how happy they were to see her out on a date. Absolutely no one said anything about that date being Reid.

He sat beside her with his arm along the back of her chair. Occasionally, he'd lean forward and whisper something in her ear. Most of the time, it was something naughty, making her blush.

She was happy the lights were down low so no one would notice. She elbowed him a few times but all he'd do was chuckle. Damn man loved to tease.

Reid stood and put his hand out to her. She gazed up at him and her stomach dropped. The man was just too sexy. She placed her hand in his and he led her to the dance floor as the band started playing the Dustin Lynch song, *Cowboys and Angels.* She put her hands on his shoulders but when he pulled her close, she linked them behind his neck and stared up at him. He smiled at her.

"Are you doing all right, Lucy?"

She grinned, feeling far more at ease than when they'd arrived. "I am. No one seems to care if we're here together."

"Why would they? Zeke's been gone over three years now, and you should be dating."

"Is that what we're doing, Reid? Dating?"

He shrugged glancing around as if he suddenly seemed self-conscious. "I suppose so. I don't know what else to call it. Do you?"

"No. But actually this is only our first date."

"True, but we've spent a lot of time together. Time I wouldn't change for the world."

"But you're going to be leaving."

"I have a farm to go back to, Lucy."

Lucy nodded. She had to be realistic because she'd always known he'd be leaving. He was just here to spend time with his family for the holidays after all, but it didn't make it any easier. Her heart was going to break when he left. She wanted him to stay, but knew she couldn't ask him to. The music stopped and the DJ announced it was almost midnight. Everyone started counting down with the clock...five...four...three...two...one.

Reid cupped her face in his hands and pressed his lips to hers. She moaned and he deepened the kiss. He raised his head slowly, staring into her eyes, and then smiled.

"Happy New Year, darlin'."

"Happy New Year, Reid. What do you say we go home?"

He nodded and took her hand in his. He led her to the coat clerk, helped her put her coat on and after shrugging into his, they walked outside to see snow coming down heavily. Lucy glanced up at the streetlights. The snow was so thick that it made the lights appear blurry. She shivered against the cold and a bit out of fear. Reid wrapped his arm around her.

"I'll get us there, don't worry."

"I know you will."

Reid helped her into the truck and she watched him walk around the front then climb in. He winked at her, and then pulled out of the parking lot to head to her ranch. It took longer than usual due to the snow accumulating on the roads. She glanced over to him and smiled. He raised an eyebrow at her.

"It looks like you're stuck with me tonight."

Reid chuckled. "I wouldn't call it being stuck with you, since I had no intention of going home tonight anyway."

Lucy grinned and glanced out the window at the snow falling around her house. God help her! She wanted this man so badly her heart ached. She watched as he climbed out of the truck and walked around to help her out. He took her hand

and led her inside the house.

"Do you want me to make a fire," he asked helping her out of her coat.

"No. Just make love to me," she whispered turning in his arms and pressing a kiss to his mouth.

Reid grinned as he took his coat and hat off. She draped the coat over a chair, and set his hat on the table before taking his hand to lead him to the bedroom. In the hallway, he tugged her to a stop and pushed her back against the wall. She stared up into his eyes.

"I want you. Here. Now," he said before taking her lips in a deep kiss.

Lucy moaned and pulled at the buttons on his shirt. He pulled it out of his jeans, pulled it over his head, and dropped it to the floor. His hands ran up her thighs and lifted her dress up around her waist. One hand moved to her panties and he dipped his hand inside, his finger moving between her slit making her whimper.

"You're wet, darlin'. Have you been thinking about this?" His words were a whisper against her ear.

"Yes," she moaned, giving herself up to his caress.

Reid's lips moved across her cheek to her lips but instead of kissing her, he took her bottom lip between his teeth and ran his tongue along it inside her mouth. Lucy fisted her hands in his hair and pulled him closer. She felt him smile against her lips before deepening the kiss and sliding his tongue into her mouth. She gasped as his finger moved between her slick, wet slit while his thumb stroked against her clitoris. She could feel she was nearing her orgasm and began to tense up when he suddenly removed his hand and dropped to his knees in front of her. She groaned with excitement when he ripped her panties from her and put one of her legs over his shoulder. She watched as he leaned close to her and ran his tongue through her curls.

"Reid..." She moaned as he continued his onslaught. She bucked against him when his teeth gently scraped against her tender flesh. His hands wrapped around her butt and pulled her closer to him. Her stomach quivered and she screamed as she came. Reid stood and kissed her mouth. She tasted her arousal on his lips. She heard his zipper go down right before he spread her legs and then he thrust into her. Hard. Lucy wrapped her legs around his waist and her arms around his neck. Her hips moved in rhythm with his. He never removed his lips from hers when she came again and he followed her over the edge, groaning into her mouth as he came. He raised his head, leaned his forehead against hers, and took deep breaths. She smiled.

"That was hot," she said and then laughed.

Reid let her down but her knees almost gave out. He caught her and leaned her against the wall. He zipped his jeans, picked her up, and carried her to the bedroom. There he stripped her out of her remaining clothes, except her boots because she'd promised to leave those on. She lay back on the bed and watched him undress, enjoying the show as he uncovered sexy muscles and by the time he'd uncovered what she wanted to see most, he was already fully aroused and eager for her again.

Reid crawled up the bed covering her body and made maddeningly slow love to her. The New Year was starting out better than any other had. Now if she could just figure out a way to get him to stay with her and Zeke, her world would be complete. With her head resting on his heaving chest and basking in the afterglow of the best lovemaking ever, Lucy let sleep pull her under.

****

Two days later, when Zeke came home, he begged Reid to take him to the barn to see his pony. Reid had decided to postpone leaving because he wasn't looking forward to leaving Lucy behind but also, because he wouldn't have had a chance to say good-bye to Zeke if he left as planned. He would have to leave soon though even if he didn't want to. He had too much to do once he got home.

"I named him Buttons. Do you like that, Reid?"

"I do. That's a good name for him," he told the boy as they entered the barn.

"I want to ride a bull someday like my daddy did," Zeke said gazing up at him.

"No, you don't. I don't want you to do that to your mom. She doesn't like the bulls." Knowing how she felt about bull riding was what kept him from telling her his plans.

"But I want to be in the rodeo." Zeke's bottom lip quivered.

"You can barrel ride. That's a good sport and fun too."

"Okay." Zeke clapped his hands. "Will you teach me?"

The time had come. The moment he'd been

dreading. Reid ran his hand down his face. "I...we'll see."

"You can come live with us and be my daddy."

Fuck! "Zeke, it's not that easy. I'm not your daddy and I have a home in another town. In fact, I've got to go home very soon."

"No! I want you to stay with us. You have to stay." Zeke wrapped his arms around Reid's legs. "I love you, Reid."

Reid picked him up and held him while he cried. *Son of a bitch!* He never should've allowed the boy to get so attached to him, but then he was just as bad. Hearing Zeke sob against his shoulder was tearing his heart out.

"I love you too, and we'll visit with each other," Reid whispered as he held the boy close. "Hey, Z-man, what do you say we go in and get some hot chocolate?"

Zeke raised his head and seeing the tears on his face just about brought Reid's tears to the surface. He sighed with relief when Zeke nodded. Reid carried him to the house but when he entered the kitchen with the boy in his arms, Lucy frowned at him when she saw the tear stains on Zeke's face.

"Is everything all right?" she asked him crossing the room to them.

Reid couldn't answer her. He knew it was going to hurt just as much to tell her he was leaving but he couldn't help but wonder if she'd have the same reaction as Zeke. Or not.

"Mama...Reid is leaving us," Zeke cried as he reached for her.

Lucy took Zeke into her arms and cradled him to her even as she glared at Reid, her eyes starting to glisten. "When?"

Her voice wasn't much louder than a whisper. He shook his head. She held Zeke until he pushed away and wanted down. Reid watched the boy run from the room.

"You knew I was leaving. Can we talk about this later? Please."

"When?" Her eyes blinked as if fighting back tears. He was hurting her. She cared enough that he was hurting her. His heart was torn between being happy that she cared and breaking her heart. He didn't want to hurt her so perhaps if they discussed this calmly, they could figure things out.

"Tomorrow." Reid ran his hand along his jaw. "Something's come up..."

"You're leaving tomorrow, and I'm just now hearing about it?"

"Actually, I've already extended my stay, Lucy."

"Then why can't you stay a bit longer. Is there a problem at your farm?"

"No."

"Reid, it's like pulling teeth with you. If there's nothing wrong, why can't you stay a while longer? Or is that you just don't want to be here any longer?" Tears filled her eyes now.

He strode to her but she stepped back, feeling like a slap. "No. Absolutely not, this has nothing to do with you or Zeke or me wanting to be here. I've loved being here with you both. There's just something I need to do..."

"What?"

"I'd rather not say right now."

She gasped, and her eyes widened allowing a

tear to slide down her cheek. "You're going to Vegas aren't you? You're going to the tribute for Zeke."

"How do you know about that?"

Lucy marched away from him, down the hallway. She returned minutes later with a letter in her hand. She thrust it at him. "They asked me to be there. I won't go. I refuse to go watch a tribute to my dead husband."

"He was a great bull rider. They do this sometimes to honor them."

"Them? Meaning men like Zeke who died in that sport? Well, I won't be a part of it."

"Well, I *am* going. I think it's great they're doing this for him, and I want to be a part of it."

"Are you riding?" When he didn't answer, she shoved him. "Is that why you're going home early...so you can prepare to try to kill yourself? Well, go then! Get out!"

Tears streamed down her cheeks even through her anger. He wanted to tell her he'd be fine.

"Lucy, please hear me out..."

"Get out," she screamed at him. "If you go there and ride, don't ever plan on coming back here." She shook her head when he reached for her.

"Lucy, I love you..." The slap she delivered to the side of his face stopped his plea.

"You don't, Reid. If you did, you wouldn't do this."

He grasped her arms and shook her. "Is this what you did to Zeke? Did you tell him not to come back if he went? Because if you did then you're right, it was your fault. Giving an

110

ultimatum like that feels like a knife to the heart, so you're as guilty of killing him as that bull." He watched as the blood drained from her face as she stared up at him. "Shit. Lucy, I'm sorry. I didn't mean that."

Her face went hard when she pushed away from him. "It doesn't matter. Just leave. We'll be fine without you."

Reid stared at her and watched her swipe at her tears. "I have to be there. This is for Zeke. You should be there too. It's an honor. It will be four years, Lucy. You could show up for that. Do it for Zeke, and your son."

"I won't. Get out," she hissed low without looking at him. He knew she meant it.

Reid turned to go and saw Zeke standing in the hallway. His face was white except for the redness of his eyes. Tears rolled down his cheeks and his chest shuddered under a sob. He turned and ran back down the hallway. Reid made a move to go after him but Lucy stepped in front of him.

"No! That is my son and I will take care of him. You have finally worn out your welcome, Reid Callahan. But know this...I love you, but I'll learn to live without you. I should be used to living without the man I love by now." She walked away from him and headed to her son's bedroom.

Torn between doing something he feels so honor bound to do, and giving it up for Lucy and Zeke was ripping Reid's heart apart. She didn't understand but he hoped she would someday. It might be too late for him but maybe she'd open her heart and mind later to benefit her son.

He picked up his Stetson, put it on his head,

and walked out slamming the kitchen door behind him. He drove to his parents' home to spend his last evening in town with family. Tomorrow morning, he'd be on his way home to prepare for one last ride. He only hoped it was worth what he'd just lost.

Chapter Eight

Reid walked through the arena, the sounds, and smells bringing back memories of good times, and bad. Several cowboys stopped him, shaking his hand, and welcoming him back. It was like coming home, only it wasn't. His best friend wasn't here, and home wasn't here anymore either. It was with Lucy and Zeke. He missed them already and only a month had passed since he'd seen them last. He shook his head. He'd thrown Zeke in her face yet she still told him she loved him. He wished she understood how important this was to him, to her husband and his friend's memory.

You're one crazy son of a bitch, Callahan. Had he thrown away the best thing ever to happen to him?

He heard his name called and he turned to see an old friend coming toward him. "Hey, Reid, how the hell are you? I heard you were going to be here. It's good to see you, man."

Lucian Black stuck his hand out to him.

"Good to see you, Luc. How have you been?"

"Great. I got married last summer."

"You? I never thought I'd see that."

Lucian laughed, slapping Reid on the shoulder. "What can I say? She won my heart."

"Is she here? I'd love to meet the woman who stole your heart."

"Oh hell, no way...I'm not introducing her to you. She's mentioned too many times how hot she thinks you are." Lucian looked him up and down. "Damned if I see it though."

Reid laughed. "Is she all right with you riding?"

"Yes, but I'm retiring the end of this year. I'm done. Getting too old for this shit."

"I hear ya. I feel the same way."

"So I hear you're riding...what bull did you draw?"

Reid clenched his jaw. "Firecracker."

"Damn. Seems fitting somehow though, doesn't it? What better way to give tribute to your best friend then for you to ride the bull that killed him. You can do this, Reid."

"I'm sure as hell going to try."

"I heard Lucy didn't come for this. That's a shame." Lucian shook his head and Reid saw the sadness in his eyes. Zeke had been well liked by all who worked the circuit.

"No, she refused to come. She hates everything about the rodeo. I wish she was here though."

Lucian grinned. "I bet you do. We all know how you felt about her, Reid. You didn't hide it very well."

Reid scowled at him. "Fuck you, Black."

Lucian laughed. "Great comeback." He slapped Reid on the back. "Good luck, buddy."

Reid watched him walk away. He really did wish that Lucy were here. If for no other reason but to prove to her, he could succeed. He huffed and continued down through the arena. He ended up at the stalls in the back and headed for Firecracker's stall. He looked in at the massive beast.

"You and I have some unfinished business,

Firecracker." Reid stared at the bull and as if he knew what he was here to do, the animal stared right back. He pawed the ground and snorted at Reid as if to say, *bring it on.* "Yeah, I don't like you either. Personally, I think you should have been hamburger by now for what you did to my best friend, but I'm going to ride your ass. You won't win this time."

Reid walked out of the back and climbed up on the fence to watch the other cowboys do their best to last eight seconds on almost eighteen hundred pounds or more of angry bull. He was getting anxious. The damn butterflies in his stomach were driving him insane. He hated the nerves that always struck him before a ride but this time was altogether different. He had to ride Firecracker and he had to succeed...for Zeke. He'd ride the bull no cowboy had stayed on for the full duration. The closest anyone ever got was Zeke, at six seconds, and he'd paid the ultimate price for that time.

Reid blew out a breath to settle his nerves. This damn bull needed to be ridden and he needed to be the man to do it.

Later when it was finally time for his ride, Reid readied himself, pulling on his glove as they loaded Firecracker into the chute. Reid stopped to tie his chaps, and then lowered his hat down low on his forehead. As he climbed up the rails and stared down at the bull, he heard the announcer tell how Zeke Albright had ridden this beast for the record time four years ago and in tribute of his best friend's life ending for that ride, Reid Callahan was going to ride Firecracker tonight. A roar went up in the arena while the other cowboys around him silently watched him. No one smiled or spoke as he straddled the bull. Firecracker jumped in the chute, snorting with anger, already trying to dislodge his rider.

Reid tuned out the sights and sounds around him as he wrapped the rope around his hand. He scooched forward on Firecracker's back and took a deep breath. He gave a terse nod to signal for the gate to be opened. This was it. *For you, Zeke.*

****

Lucy sat on the edge of her seat, silently praying as she watched the gate swing open. Firecracker jumped out of the chute and kicked his back legs high in the air as he tried to rid himself of Reid from his back. Time stood still, and her heart climbed into her throat as she watched the bull jump one way, and then the other. She still wasn't sure why she came tonight except that she had to know. If he was able to do it, she wanted to be here. If the worst happened, she wanted to know it had, not hear about it later.

She'd cried for days after Reid left and cursed herself over, and over again for pushing him away. Maybe he was more right about her and Zeke than she'd ever admitted to herself before. She'd pushed Reid from her life because he wanted to do what he loved in memory of her dead husband who'd died doing what he loved. She'd decided it was selfish of her to tell him he couldn't ride so now she was here to see what happened when he did. If he made it through alive, she was going to apologize and try to make it up to him...if he'd let her.

With the crowd cheering, Reid stayed on with

his arm high in the air, his body racked from side to side, and forward to back. Firecracker spun in circles, furiously trying to throw his rider. Lucy held her breath, and when she glanced up at the clock, her belly clutched. Six seconds, he'd reached Zeke's time but then she realized Reid was still on at seven, and then eight.

The buzzer rang and the crowd roared. Lucy stood along with the crowd, knowing the danger wasn't over. Reid needed to get clear of the bull. She wrung her hands as she watched as Reid untied his hand before jumping off the bull and landing on his feet. When Firecracker ran for him, Reid took off for the fence jumping it before the bull rammed it. *He did it!*

The other cowboys surrounded Reid, slapping him on the back with congratulations while the rodeo clowns corralled Firecracker from the arena. Reid hopped back over the fence now that it was safe, ran to the center of the floor, and threw his hat up in the air. He raised his hands in the air and looked up at the ceiling then he dropped to one knee, and hung his head as if in prayer. Lucy wondered if he was talking to Zeke. Tears ran down Lucy's face as she applauded along with the entire arena as he took a few more bows and accepted the crowd's ovation.

She moved from her seat and ran down the metal stairs to the back of the arena. She needed to see him, to acknowledge what he'd done and why. She needed to see him to make sure he really was okay. When she found Reid, cowboys and buckle bunnies surrounded him. A couple of the gals were already trying to gain his attention to boost their own.

Oh hell no! Not going to happen!

Lucy made her way through the crowd and when she was close enough, said his name. He spun around and stared at her, his eyes wide as if he thought he was seeing things. She smiled.

"Lucy?" He started toward her, and everyone parted to let him get to her.

"You did it." Her heart was pounding in her chest and she wanted to throw herself into his arms but didn't dare...not after the way she'd treated him.

"I...yes, I did," he said with a proud grin. "What are you doing here?"

"I had to see, Reid. I just had to know. I had to see you do it."

Reid pulled her into his arms, kissed her, and held onto her as if his life depended on it. She knew hers did. She wrapped her arms around his waist and cried against his shoulder.

"I'm so sorry," she exclaimed, her voice hoarse and cracking through sobs. "I shouldn't have said the things I did. I'm sorry I slapped you."

"It's all right. We both said things we shouldn't have." He pulled back from her and cupped her face in his hands. "But I meant one of those things, Lucy. I love you. I love you so much...you and Zeke. I want to marry you, and the three of us be a family. I'll keep my farm and let someone else run it so Zeke always knows where home is and we can go there once in a while for visits."

"I want that too...sounds perfect," she whispered.

Reid leaned down and kissed her. Applause erupted around them. Lucy glanced around, having forgotten where they were. All the cowboys and even the buckle bunnies were clapping and cheering. She smiled, feeling a blush spread over her face. "I think they approve."

Reid laughed and nodded. "That's all we need then, right?" He kissed her forehead. "Let's go home. This was my last ride, and that's a promise."

Lucy hugged him. "If you're sure."

"I'm positive, darlin'. Nothing is as important to me as you and Zeke, and whatever our future brings us..." He leaned down close. "I'm going to enjoy working on siblings for our boy."

She grinned up at him. She liked him thinking of Zeke as their son. "You are a naughty cowboy but I do love you, Reid Callahan. Let's go home."

****

Reid stared down at the headstone then took his hat off, and squatted down. He spun the brim in his hand. He took a deep breath and blew it out making a puff of air in front of him.

"Hey, buddy. I still miss you. I'm not sure if you can hear me, but I have to talk to you. I'm...I'm in love with Lucy and Zeke. I want them to be my family. I promise you that I'll take care of them for the rest of my days." He glanced up at the gray skies. "I rode that son of a bitch, Zeke. I rode Firecracker the full eight seconds. I heard they're retiring him. I went out a winner and he went out a loser. I just wish it had been you." He stood but didn't leave. He glanced around the cemetery. He was the only one out here on such a cold, dreary February day. Flurries flew around him and the wind howled. He had to be here though. He needed to talk to Zeke.

"I've asked Lucy to marry me, Zeke. I've always loved her but I need your blessing, buddy. I have to know you're all right with this. Of course, I have no idea how you're going to let me know. Lucy deserves to be happy, and I promise I can make her and Zeke happy." Reid grinned thinking how she'd told him he was the best present she'd ever received—a cowboy for Christmas.

"How can you let me know you're fine with this? Damn, Zeke. I promise I'll be good to her and Z-man. I didn't think I could ever love two people so much. They're my life. Come on, Zeke. Let me know, somehow." He stood there staring at the headstone not really expecting any kind of answer when all of a sudden, the clouds parted, and a sliver of sunlight shone down on the headstone then moved over Reid. A shiver as if someone had passed by him made him look up. He grinned, put his hat on, and tapped the brim. "Thanks, Zeke."

* *The End* *

About the Author

Susan was born and raised in Cumberland, MD. She moved to Tennessee in 1996 with her husband and they now live in a small town outside of Nashville, along with their three dogs. She is a huge Nashville Predators hockey fan. She also enjoys fishing, taking drives down back roads, and visiting Gatlinburg, TN, her family in Pittsburgh, PA, and her hometown. Although Susan's books are a series, each book can be read as standalone books. Each book will end with a HEA and a new story beginning in the next one. She would love to hear from her readers and promises to try to respond to all.

You can visit her Facebook page and website by the links below.

https://www.facebook.com/skdromanceauthor

www.susanfisherdavisauthor.weebly.com

Email: susan@susanfisherdavisauthor.com

Made in the USA
Monee, IL
10 November 2022